Fresh, Green Life

Fresh, Green Life

A NOVEL

Sebastian Castillo

SOFT SKULL
NEW YORK

Fresh, Green Life

First Soft Skull edition: 2025

Library of Congress Cataloging-in-Publication Data
Names: Castillo, Sebastian, 1988- author.
Title: Fresh, green life : a novel / Sebastian Castillo.
Description: First Soft Skull edition. | New York : Soft Skull, 2025.
Identifiers: LCCN 2025000353 | ISBN 9781593767914 (trade paperback) | ISBN 9781593767921 (ebook)
Subjects: LCGFT: Novels.
Classification: LCC PS3603.A877 F74 2025 | DDC 813/.6—dc23/eng/20250107
LC record available at https://lccn.loc.gov/2025000353

Cover design by Kit Schluter
Book design by Olenka Burgess

Soft Skull Press
New York, NY
www.softskull.com

Printed in the United States of America

10 9 8 7 6 5 4 3 2 1

You must change your life.
—RAINER MARIA RILKE

Nobody can counsel and help you, nobody.
—RAINER MARIA RILKE

Contents

BEGGING   · 3 ·

CRYING   · 69 ·

Acknowledgments   · 143 ·

Fresh, Green Life

Begging

I had considered my options throughout the day, at first thinking I would spend New Year's Eve alone in my apartment, getting drunk off beer and watching videos, then admitting this too depressing a solution to my evening, perhaps coloring the forthcoming year in a somewhat inauspicious light. I then thought of taking the Amtrak up to New York to watch the ball drop at Times Square, cheering down time among the jubilant throng, those perennial revelers whom I had only ever witnessed as anonymous holiday extras on the television screen. The possibility of transforming myself into one of those people for the evening felt attractive enough to justify the expensive train ride and long evening in the cold, though, it was true, the few friends I had who lived in that city likely had other plans, and if I were to find a place to sleep after the ball had dropped, I would have to arrange something quickly. My final option was to spend New Year's Eve at Professor Aleister's, as he had emailed me a few days prior, first to apologize for allowing such a long gap in our admittedly seldom correspondence, and then to say he was throwing a party at his home in the Philadelphia suburbs, adding, in a somewhat overly familiar way, I thought, that even though he was now alone and a widower, he wouldn't let that get in the way of enjoying the little time he likely had left in his life. He had never previously mentioned that his wife had died. At the end of his email he said that several of my graduating year's cohort from the philosophy and literature department would be in attendance, and that should I like to see what Robert, Thomas, and *Maria* (he had italicized her name) had been doing in the decade since our graduation, I should think about spending the evening at his house, although, he admitted, it was a somewhat unorthodox gathering to begin with, but one that he felt was necessary to hold, given his more-recent-than-not retirement from teaching—he had never had a retirement party proper—and of course, his even more recently passed birthday on Christmas Day, adding that he had always, throughout his life, felt cheated of a decent birthday party due to this natal coincidence. The gathering would therefore offer itself thrice over: a celebration of a retirement, a birthday, and a New Year, in that order. I reread the invitation as many times, and couldn't help but notice Professor Aleister's italicization of Maria's purported presence: perhaps he knew how I had felt about her all throughout my schooling years, how I had never done a thing about it, not once, and how possibly that fondness had still not dampened over the years. And how furthermore there is perhaps no greater excitement than seeing an old love interest yet again, years later, with the hope of advancing what was not possible before. This is especially true if one is more lissome and statuesque than when last seeing that never-to-be beloved, which as it happens was precisely the case with me. I am no model, surely, but in the past several years I've taken an utmost interest in my health after a minor heart scare, a heart scare that should not have happened at my age, and I consequently began exercising six days a week, eating the healthiest and most organic food I could afford with my meager teacher's salary, and finally, giving up cigarette smoking. The sum effect of this, course, was that while my body was once unflattering and general—marked by all manner of playtime excess—it was now lithe, muscular, and cast by the daily work that gave it shape. I had made myself a sculpture. Even my skin appeared more limpid than it did when I was in my twenties, when I was always on some badly cut party drug, chain-smoking yellow American Spirits, and shoving late-night, grease-dripping food into my mouth. The consummate diet of the young academic, as it were. Yes, the Professor had left this detail of Maria dangling in his email—surely, he knew what he was doing—and as I was long-lonesomely single and desperate to capture her attention, he knew I would likely come, and he was right.

I discovered through social media that Maria had recently divorced from her consultant husband, whom I remember she had met during a summer internship for the United Nations. She was working with a department having to do with the business of South Korea, whatever that business may have been, and one day during her lunch break she had encountered a young brutish man (I say he is brutish, at least) who was at the time working for the French consulate. This was the summer before our final year at school, at our dear, experimental liberal arts college in the outskirts of the greater Philadelphia area. We were sweating at our cramped wooden desks on our first day back from summer break, in that Hobbit-like stone hermitage which often housed our philosophy classes, when Maria had told me this, how she had met this Andrei, a Russian American man from New Jersey who studied French, and how they started dating from the day they met, and were now maintaining a long-distance relationship—Pennsylvania to New York, at least—and how she decided that, no matter what happened regarding her future employment, she would be moving to New York City once we had finished that final year of schooling. She had always wanted to move to New York, she added, where *things really happened*. Things only seemed to happen in Philadelphia, or rather, things happened much like they happened elsewhere: indifferently and without mention. In New York, however, everyday events took on a totemic importance, and were immediately enshrined in a documentary-like collective memory among all who lived there. It is perhaps for this reason there are so many movies about that city. I remember, too, having felt a shock when she told me about her new relationship: this boy's full name was the same as that of my favorite film, about the eponymous fifteenth-century Russian painter of icons. As she finished announcing this news to me, Professor Aleister walked into our sweltering classroom, visibly sweating through a thick cable-knit sweater he wore year-round, regardless of the weather. It seemed as well he was not wont to wash it, as there were always deeply discolored brown splotches at his armpits—stark as ink stains against the sweater's beige—scandalously on display when he lifted his arms to write something on the chalkboard. Maria and I had enrolled in Professor Aleister's class on Dante's *Divine Comedy*—though he was to refer to it only as "La commedia"—which was listed by our university as a course of philosophy, and not of literature. Given the experimental nature of our school, strict distinctions of academic genre were often not properly abided, and as such one could take a course on, say, the occult economies of sub-Saharan Africa, and this would be listed as a course in literature, not in economics or sociology. And just the same, one could take a course titled, say, "Balzac's Nineteenth

Century," and one would find oneself in a course regarding the post-Revolutionary political economy of France, and not, in any way, literature. It would be possible that one would not read the name Balzac anywhere that semester outside of what was printed on the front page of the course syllabus. Our school lacked proper majors as well, so that when one went gallivanting in the city of Philadelphia and mingled with the students of Temple University or the University of Pennsylvania, and those same inquisitive students posed questions regarding one's major, the students of our school often found themselves in a position to craft roundabout speeches explaining how they didn't have "real majors," as it were, but "academic concentrations," and these concentrations in turn reflected more refined scholarly interests that could not quite be reduced to a "literature major" or a "psychology major," though often enough, after a year or two of these speeches, many of us would forgo such perfunctory explanations and simply concede that, indeed, they "majored" in philosophy and literature, as was the case with me, as well as with Maria, Robert, and Thomas. Yes, on that first day back from summer break, Professor Aleister walked in and without so much as a deferential nod toward any of us wrote a line of poetry on the board—from Eliot's *Four Quartets*: "The wisdom only the knowledge of dead secrets"—and said this single line of poetry would function as our "syllabus" for the semester. There would be no other course policy or instructions. He then spent the rest of the class period asking each of us in turn to discern what he could possibly mean by this—how a line of poetry, from Eliot no less, could function as the course syllabus on the teaching of Dante's writing, which was in fact a class of philosophy, moral philosophy, the Professor emphasized, and not of literature. The Professor did this every semester. One semester, our "syllabus" was a line from Frost: "We dance round in a ring and suppose / But the Secret sits in the middle and knows." Another semester, it was from Emerson: "Everything looks permanent until its secret is known." And so on with secrets. It was for this reason I had taken classes with Professor Aleister, and why the few of us (such as Maria, Thomas, and Robert) had returned to him so often: we would barely do any work. Professor Aleister often came in with a quote, with a print cutting from some review or article, and he would lead us into argument among ourselves without any real reason or, by the end of that period, any satisfying conclusion as to why we had passed seventy minutes in the manner we had. That Dante course was my seventh with the Professor, under whom I ultimately studied for four years, lazily and haphazardly reading Aristotle, Augustine, Descartes, Hegel (who he was made to teach against his will, he said), and a variety of Gnostic lunatics. Well over ten years had now passed since this period, and I could scarcely tell you much about what any of these men had written down in their famous books I was put to read and which later I was asked to write about at a length of ten to twenty pages, essays I had completed always at the very last possible moment, because their quality did not matter. I unequivocally received an A– on these assignments: *strong ideas, as always*, the Professor's remarks would say, *but needs work in execution*. I was certain he did not read them beyond the titles, which, I admit, I had put great effort into fashioning as clever puns: something like, "Nasty Kant: Gender, Affective Altruism, and the Categorical Imperative."

That Dante course would be the last I shared with Maria. In this final class, the Professor kept returning to a certain line from Dante, which he would always cite in the Italian, despite the fact he never otherwise did this with any other line from the book: *E caddi come corpo morto cade.* He said this was the key to Dante: *And I fell, like a dead body falls.* In Canto V, Dante encounters Paolo and Francesca, the ill-fated lovers damned to the second circle of Hell in an eternal whirlwind. After Dante hears their story, he faints. I remember the Professor said all of Dante could be conjured in this image—that the world of Dante was the world of fainting, of total syncope, so unable are we to bear the stories other people tell us. We are all forever being thrown off a cliff, in Italian. And moreover, in the original, the Professor said, Dante offers us the striking insistence of those alliterative C's: *E caddi come corpo morto cade,* which he said sounded like an infirm pebble banging against a rock. That lecture ended, I remember, with the Professor's remark that we were all infirm pebbles, tumbling downwardly to the mouth of Hell, and often throughout the rest of the course he would walk into the classroom muttering *E caddi come corpo morto cade* in such a low and gravelly patter that it sounded like a percussive jingle intended to threaten us. Before opera and poetry, he said, Italian was the language of damnation.

The following semester, our last, was dedicated to writing our thesis projects and the private, library research they demanded, which meant that most of us either did nothing or got drunk for a living. Soon enough our graduation came, and the light occupational camaraderie our cohort had developed more or less ceased to be, as is often the case when one departs from the institution that binds a group, though we would all occasionally send one another dutiful emails or texts for birthdays, holidays, and the like. As one can imagine, those intermittent messages became less frequent as the years proceeded. Maria moved to New York as she had promised, where she soon married, a development I found lightly wretched. I admit to keeping track of her throughout the years. Though I never met the man, I learned much about Andrei through this passive, social-media-abetted endeavor of mine: he loved pit bulls, for example, which had led to their adopting of one; he also very much enjoyed riding a bicycle, and wearing the absurd, bright latex clothing of a cyclist while doing so. Before their relationship, I had never heard Maria discuss the using of bicycles for any purpose. It seemed Andrei had been successful in convincing her of the pleasures in the activity, for only a few months into their relationship Maria would regularly post images of the two of them riding their bicycles, entering various races and tournaments and so on. Maria, at least for a period, seemed to have been wholly consumed by the activity, as she would often post photographs of newly acquired bicycle gear or indeed new bicycles themselves, as well as various routes she had found in the New York City area, such as along the Bronx River Parkway, and sometimes as far north as the upper reaches of Westchester and Putnam Counties, which, I estimate, must have taken several hours to reach from her Brooklyn apartment. I also learned that Andrei was quite the amateur cook— he created a separate social media account dedicated to his off-beat variations on classic dishes, such as a cacio e pepe topped with the grated dust of Flaming Hot Cheetos. I never "followed" this account, of course—that would have been a transgression, given the fact I did not formally know this man— but I would regularly return to view it, as Andrei was keen to post pictures of not just his food, but of Maria as well, tasting these concoctions, as she, I presumed, was his chief recipe tester, if not his entire gustatory audience. There they often were:

Maria and the pit bull in the background of these photos, dreamily gazing at their beloved chef. It is not surprising, of course, that I detested every facet of this man. I hated his bland, stock-photo face, his haute young-professional leisure-wear monochrome wardrobe, and his style of internet posting, which felt clueless—without an ounce of depth or character yet simultaneously try-hard. I found it utterly unacceptable that he shared a name with my favorite movie, which to this day I have been unable to revisit because of the associations I now had with it. I hated how he seemed almost a caricature of bourgeois urban success: he a man who for an over-handsome living sends corporate emails of no consequence, who photographs himself smiling infant-like at industrial breweries on the weekends, and who professes the most anodyne opinions on the latest bottom-gutter consumer media product as soon as the culture had induced him to do so. And worst of all, I hated how easily Maria had fitted herself into that quotidian image of youthful-yet, thirtysomething satisfaction. It would not be untrue to say I had wished, to some degree, for the dissolution of their union, however unlikely it may have seemed throughout the years. So, it was both to my delight and surprise that I detected a subtle shift in the kinds of images Maria began posting in recent months. Whereas in the past, when Maria had posted a photograph of herself, it was always with Andrei, or perhaps with a friend with whom she was celebrating a birthday. Occasionally she posed with the dog in some family member's backyard, though more often than not the dog appeared in these photographs on his own. Now she had taken to posting photos of herself alone. She looked as charming and as devastating as ever, if not, I had noticed, *even more so*. It was in her clothing, in how she held herself, in the angling of the photograph: all invited a sense of awe and astonishment. Whereas I had never "liked" the photographs of her and Andrei—for, of course, I did not in any way *like* them—I now found myself "liking" all of these photographs of Maria *isolé*. Then, three months ago, she announced what I, and perhaps many of us who followed her internet activity from afar, had suspected: she had gotten a divorce. Andrei had accepted a job offer in Los Angeles; he had taken the dog to that sunny and vacuous side of the world. I had a pressing desire to know more—was he, deep down, for example, an exceptionally selfish and stupid person, utterly unsuited for adult companionship, and who therefore deserved the absolute worst of the world, etc.?—but the details didn't matter. This announcement felt to me akin to the granting of some long-sought-after wish received by token of a patron saint to whom one did not know they were praying. Immediately I put my mind to crafting excuses for how I could reach out to her, with the hopes of organizing some casual meeting where we could discuss how our lives had gone in the long stretch since we had last seen each other, whereupon I would feign surprise to hear about her recent breakup, offering a general condolence which would then transform into a commiseration of past exes, breaking the ground for something beyond the friendship we had so enjoyed during our years at school. The trouble, of course, was that I had not seen Maria in several years. Our cohort had kept up the ritual of desultory invitations to things, but neither Maria nor I had ever been able commit to these gatherings—either she could not make it down to Philadelphia, or I to New York, and of course, these invitations were always extended with the pretext that they would be occasions to spend time not just with each other, but the whole cadre from our school, since the majority of us had either stayed in Philadelphia, or, like Maria, moved to one of the lesser-expensive boroughs of New York City. Our relationship had remained a digitally epistolary one, often in the exchange of small, short jokes sent to each other in response to photographs or postings we had made on our various social media accounts. So: if I had come out and messaged Maria about a long-overdue meetup *now*, it would seem remarkably obvious what I was doing. One of the things that had long endeared me to her was her uncanny perceptiveness, and her Rabelaisian sense of humor. I could see her making a joke right away: *So, you're finally going to try to fuck me, book man?*

An evening at Professor Aleister's seemed to me the perfect and most delicate point of entry for what I desired. Not sex, I should establish, but a more expressive and expansive meeting with Maria: a reclamation of the familiar, a recuperation of the lightly gone past. During our tenure at the university, Professor Aleister had often invited me and the rest of the philosophy cohort over to his house for dinner or drink, as it was walking distance from our idyllic suburban campus. The Professor wished to know us on a *spiritual level*, he said, a sort of intimacy that is simply forbidden at the institutional stratum, no matter how much the pageantry of the liberal arts classroom suggested otherwise. He said that the matter of philosophy was not simply a matter of the mind, of abstract thinking and of building concepts, but of the body, too, of the body and of the heart and of the spirit, as he put it (I would never use such language), and that one could not get to philosophy with another person until they had sat across from each other and shared plates, cups, and knives. As poor twentysomethings, we were more than delighted to consume what we would otherwise not have had the chance to sample—steak tartare paired with some particularly fragrant Beaujolais, or duck terrine with an over-full negroni. The Professor, for all his demerits, was generous with his drink and victuals. But we soon discovered these occasional visits to the Professor's house were merely an excuse for him to yet again be granted an audience. The classroom, where, after all, he was by definition saddled with a pedagogical task, however halfheartedly executed, was not enough. He needed a real arena for discussion, where, as he put it, anything and everything went, nothing was beyond reproach, no topic was condemned. We would not have spent a minute longer there than we would have needed had we not been plied with European-seeming food and expensive alcohol. We would, for the most part, sit there quietly as the Professor carried forth, always deeper into more thematically questionable topics. Once, for example, when discussing Ancient Greek and Hellenistic philosophy, he wondered aloud, *following the way of life put forward by the Socratic method*, as he put it, whether a person could be considered a student unless they had been fucked in the ass by their teacher. I remember Robert, Thomas, and I staring down into our cups when the Professor said this, feeling the heat of impropriety rush to my face. I looked up and saw, to my surprise, Maria smiling beatifically, as if expecting this line of thinking from the Professor, and slowly developing her response in turn. We all understood the Professor deeply enjoyed these moments—saying what he knew he shouldn't, whether he even meant what it was he was saying—because it demonstrated, deep down, he was the type of person who would cross a certain social threshold. He was not a simpering, pusillanimous coward, like the rest of the Humanities faculty, but a real maverick—it proved, so he thought, that he was not beholden to anything beyond his temperament. In those moments at Professor Aleister's home, it was only Maria who had the gumption to respond to him. Professor, she said, if that's the case, what happens when a student fucks their teacher in the ass? We laughed, of course, but the Professor did not take to these rejoinders as mirthfully: *that has never happened in the history of education,* he said, and with that, bid us good night. This was no isolated incident. Maria was fearless, whereas the rest of us met the stereotype of young men of philosophy and literature: meek, passive-aggressive, and socially impotent. At the time, I had thought that perhaps because Maria was the only woman in our cohort, she felt the need to demonstrate some daring in the face of Professor Aleister's provocations as "a credit to her gender" (another of the Professor's phrases). But I was wrong, and had assumed incorrectly: she did so because she found it fun. Whereas I (or Robert or Thomas) frequented the Professor's because the free food and drink seemed a fair exchange to be cudgeled by talk, Maria desired a true sparring partner. In the classroom, Maria kept quiet, taking notes and asking for further elucidation on some finer points in our course texts. At the Professor's house, however, she was purely polemical. She had always found it startling how, in the classroom, the men of our cohort (myself included, she added) would feel perfectly comfortable blathering on about things we knew very little about. *Most of you don't even do the reading!* she would tease, and it was true. For Maria, the classroom was the place for clarification, not for holding forth. The Professor's house, she said to me one night when we were drunkenly walking back to our respective dorms, was her opportunity to advance what she had acquired through her reading, her study, her listening. She wanted to feel she was able to speak as plainly and convincingly as possible. She had noticed, she said, that whenever Robert or Thomas or I (or the Professor!) were challenged, or unable to come up with an adequate response for a gap in our reasoning, our speech became infinitely more complex and laden with the sorts of neologisms endemic to academic philosophy as a field. The more our speech mimicked that of an eighteenth-century German Idealist, she had said, the less we knew what it was we were talking about. It was, to her, a great pleasure to feel in every way the intellectual superior in those situations, and keep quiet till her tête-a-têtes at Professor Aleister's house, when she could leave everyone with their tongues growing ever fatter in their mouths.

She must have gotten this out of her system, for in the last week at our dear experimental liberal arts college on the outskirts of Philadelphia, Maria said she would never read a book of philosophy again. It was a trifling though admittedly diverting joy, I remember her saying, and now it was time to return to real life. Philosophy was, decidedly, not a component of that. And I must admit, it is for this reason I felt somewhat skeptical when rereading the Professor's invitation for the evening. I could see Robert and Thomas spending their New Year's Eve at a former teacher's house. They continued to live in the Philadelphia area, after all, and if I recalled correctly, they were both absolute fucking losers. Robert with his hair, Thomas with his shirts. I liked them, of course, but it was the truth. So while it was easy to imagine those two sitting once more as a mute pair under Professor Aleister's discursive assault—though perhaps that assault would have softened now, as he would be in his mid-eighties—it was much more difficult to imagine Maria permitting the same for herself. On Christmas Eve, I did see she had posted a picture from her childhood home in Bala Cynwyd, which was not so very far from the Professor's house. It's possible that, in the immediate fallout of her divorce, she had decided to recover under the auspices of her family's home, and her doting mother and father, whom I met only once, on the day of our graduation, whom I remembered being the very picture of familial support—pillars of cheer, tenderness, and appropriate suburban enthusiasm. And if Maria was spending such an extended holiday period in that convalescent atmosphere, it was perhaps just as likely she would opt to spend an hour or two at the Professor's house, to once again share time among old friends for a few holiday drinks, before returning to her parents' house for a quiet night, a New Year's Eve where one barely manages to make it to midnight, where the television bleats its Times Square crystalball countdown like an annual duty it must return to once more. She'd hug her parents, give each a light kiss on the forehead, and wish them good night. She would then sleep in her childhood bedroom, which had more or less been converted into an office space for her father, whom, if I recalled correctly, worked from home as some sort of actuarial accountant. While in that room there was now a filing cabinet and a desk cluttered with notebooks and papers and a dusty Dell computer, it would still retain a certain character that would remind her of the early adolescent things she had first experienced in that very room, and as she was going to sleep for the first time in the new year, she would feel greeted by a comforting past that was, despite all her hardships, still there for her when she most needed it in the year to come.

It was entirely possible this was the course Maria had set for herself that evening, and that Professor Aleister was being truthful in his email—suggesting that if anything might change the course of that seemingly predetermined outcome, it could be me. She would be preparing to announce her departure from Professor Aleister's, and at that moment I would convince her against returning to her parents' home, and instead suggest she spend the rest of her New Year's Eve back in Philadelphia proper. We would be sitting there at the Professor's house, half ignoring whatever blithering argot the Professor was going on about, when I would turn toward Maria, conspiratorially, and say: Wouldn't it be nice to get out of here and visit one of our old haunts back in Philadelphia? They were likely open late, I would say, due to it being New Year's Eve and all, and not only that, I would even spring for a cab to get us there. Maybe we could go to El Bar? Or how about Dirty Frank's? And wasn't that such a nice time, that one night at Dirty Frank's during our senior year, when a dog somehow made its way into the bar—a complete stray—and we managed to coax the mutt into our corner, taking him into our care while the bartender called the SPCA to come and cart the dog off to the pound? And remember how, for the course of a week or two, we pretended we had adopted the dog—we even gave him a name, Logos—and that he was now under our joint stewardship? This never came to be, of course. We had merely adopted poor Logos in our imagination! But do you remember how I would text you something like: Do you think Logos has been a good boy today? And you would respond, Oh, yes, Logos has been a good boy. Do you really think so? I would say, and you would say, Our little Logos has been a very good boy indeed.

Yes: Maria and I could spend a whole evening sharing a conversation of this nature, recalling events such as the adoption of our little Logos. And maybe, after a few further drinks, Maria would let slip some admiration. She would say: Sorry if this is stupid, but Sebastián, you look different! And I would, of course, then deliver a speech I had more or less drafted in my mind about the decisions I had made for myself in the past several years. I would say: It was only with great difficulty that I had come to possess the current changes in my body that you note tonight, Maria. One might call my physique *admirable*, but I would not. In fact, one evening, after a particularly vigorous workout, there I stood in the academy locker room (yes, I call my gymnasium *the academy*, like the Portuguese—for the academy is not merely a place to cultivate the mind, but the body, too), and I was inspecting my physique in the mirror, completely in the nude. I stood before the mirror when an older fellow walked past me, who, as it turned out, was inspecting my body as well. And this older man said: Quite the admirable body you have there. And to him I said: A body cannot be admirable. Merely possessing a body, which, as far as I can tell, is a prerequisite for living as we know it, should not inspire admiration in any person. It can inspire shame, Maria, of course it can, we all but know this too well: the original sin of existing, of nakedness, of all the blood and pus produced by our holes. All these disgusting liquids that want to get out of us. But to replace that shame with admiration is to play into the very game that shame metes out. Merely applying its inverse will do no one any good, God help us. We should instead prepare an indifference toward the body, a moral and aesthetic apathy. I would say to Maria that I had said this to that older man who was admiring me, that yes, while some might call my body, after several thousand hours of exercise, admirable, I would not. And I would say to Maria that I had begun this activity due to an unexpected heart scare, a heart scare that should not have happened at my age, and it was then that I became a person who commits himself to health exercises. For most of my life, I would say, I had felt that I should be someone who commits himself to such a thing. That I should be a person who wakes up and knows that at some point in their day, at some hour scheduled into their daily program, they will perform an activity known as health exercises. I would become someone who knew that success in life, indeed in personhood itself, depended on whether they would submit themselves to such an activity. I would ascend ever upward in my life, all thanks to the beneficent results of moving in such a manner wherein my heart rate would climb above its resting pulse; I would move in such a way that my movement would induce traumas to my muscle fibers, which would then rebuild themselves and overcompensate during that process, so that they would become larger as a result. I would become larger. But the key thing, I would say to Maria, was that I was not doing this in order to create a physique that *some might call admirable*. No. Instead, regularly performing these health exercises would speak deeply to the sensibility I had developed within myself, and to what this sensibility said of my character writ large. That is, I would so deeply become myself—*the real version of myself who I should have been all along, who knew how to live*—that I would transform from person (inadequate) to character (good). Though I am an atheist, I can say with certainty that God prefers archetypes to individuals. They wrote the Bible as they did for a reason.

It was like this, I would repeat to Maria, through a commitment to the thing they refer to as health exercises, that I had come to appear as I

did, and why I, as Maria would put it, looked "different." And all this great effort was to say: Look
at what I have done to make myself better. Maria
would then be put into a position to think: *Look
at how Sebastián has changed, how he is different, yes,
yes, how much better he's become. Oh! And how good
of him, how incredibly good of him.* We would be sitting in Dirty Frank's again or maybe up north at
El Bar, and she would find herself gazing into me,
after I had delivered my speech, reconsidering the
nature of what had transpired between us up to
that point, reorganizing the contents of her memories, recasting and shifting them. Something would
change within her. The forthcoming year, which she
had imagined as a period of adjusting to the newfound, lonely difficulty of life after marriage, would
be rendered in an entirely different nature. It would
not be bogged by the vagaries of independent suffer-
ing, but instead would have a clearer pronunciation,
one that sounded like my name, which I had legally
changed to include an accent on the *a*—to prove I
had ascended well past the person I once was.

So it was not entirely far-fetched, I found myself repeating while showering in preparation for
the evening, not so entirely far-fetched, for Maria

to spend a part of her New Year's Eve at Professor Aleister's. I could see her there clearly, in fact, installed amid Robert and Thomas and me, listening to the old man go on about some contemporary rival in philosophy or literature who had just published a book that wasn't very good, that didn't deserve the attention or accolades it had received from the academic or general public. This was the position the Professor often took with the work of other academics. So-and-so's new paper on Schopenhauer's family correspondence was middling, he would say, or someone or other's recent essay collection on neoliberalism and Stoic thought was worth less than the paper on which it was printed. I had always found this odd, of course, because the Professor himself had written so little in his life. He had published a few papers at the beginning of his career, and a single study on Schiller—or was it Schlegel? (Certainly not Hegel!) Nevertheless, after receiving tenure, he had ceased publishing original work completely. He continued as a more-or-less decently respected translator of Spanish and Italian, but these translations he put out perhaps once a decade. I imagined, now that I myself worked at a university and am a professor in my own right—albeit as a contingent instructor, an adjunct, a classroom garbage man—that there was pressure from his department for Professor Aleister to continue in the academic labor that was required of him: to put out, at least once every few years, some original writing or research that absolutely no one would ever read, but which would be necessary social theater for his station as a professor of philosophy and literature at a vaguely prestigious, experimental liberal arts university on the outskirts of Philadelphia. How he had evaded this injunction was a mystery to me. It is, most likely, a generational difference in our labor market—once upon a time, professors had to do little else but show up to their classes and dutifully carry out their small responsibilities among their students. Now professors were expected to have published a mountain of work by the age of thirty, to have led such-and-such a panel, and delivered several papers at conferences, before even being considered for the worst-paying, most-overworked position in their industry. Such is the case when a profession has imploded and is regarded with general distrust—if not outright disgust—by the public. Everyone hates college professors, who indeed are largely insufferable, untalented people.

Professor Aleister had gotten through the life of an academic at the tail end of an era where one was given quite a bit of freedom in and outside of the classroom. It was a perfect job, it must be said, for the incredibly lazy.

After graduating, the Professor and I maintained a correspondence over email. I was, after all, his star pupil, or so he said. I remember, in my last year, his repeated urging that after graduating I should continue into graduate school to earn a doctorate in philosophy, as he thought I had the necessary grit (and it was implied, delusion) to attempt such a thing. This was based, I imagined then and now, on my contributions to classroom discussions, and nothing else. Professor Aleister would again come in with a quotation—his fundamental genre was the aphorism, as they are short and generally have the effect of making their reader feel very smart for little effort—and after reading this quote aloud to us and writing it on the board, he would ask us what the author could mean by this. After hearing what a few of my peers had to say, I would typically find some ulterior, antithetical way of reading what was provided—I sought the counterintuitive explanation, challenging the limits of basic literacy, as

I had discovered this was often the best and most impressive strategy for academic close readings. Once, for example, the Professor shared with us something from Nietzsche: "Three anecdotes are enough to give the picture of a person." The Professor sat back in his chair after sharing this, appearing satisfied with himself, as if he had provided us with a quotation he believed half of us would remember for the rest of our lives. Professor Aleister then asked: What could he possibly mean by this? Three anecdotes? That's it? The picture of a person? I remember then Roger's hand shot up, and most of us in the room flinched. Roger was in the year below mine, and it seemed he was often in a tacit duel with Professor Aleister to be the most irritating, unbearable person in the room. Roger raised his hand, and without being called on, said, "But can't you argue that *three* anecdotes is not enough? Why not four? And maybe you only need one. Maybe only one is enough." Roger seemed to me a sort of prototype of a certain intellectual boy—one whose sole reason for occupying himself with the matter of philosophy, of literature, was so that he could explain something about it to anyone who would listen: either the author was deficient, or the author's readers, or most often, both. And so in his typical kvetching custom, Roger aimed his sights on Nietzsche, first explaining that the quote provided to us was indeed speciously formulated, inarticulate, and perhaps did not merit sharing in the classroom. And the Professor, barely hiding his disdain for the boy, spoke through his teeth: *Say more*, he said. This was a trick I learned from the Professor once I myself had become a teacher—the easiest way to minimize one's work in the classroom was to ask students to say more. Say more, please—there is always more to say! And Roger did. Was the *number* really so important? he repeated. And the Professor said perhaps it both was and it wasn't. Roger then looked as if he had won something. If he could get the Professor to admit that the number wasn't so important—though he had not yet committed to this possibility—then it seemed Roger would be justified with his needling, and would have, once more, proved to himself, and to all of us, his supremacy in matters of philosophy and literature, his role as the resident sage on matters of the mind. In this manner, we could easily lose an hour of class time if Roger was in attendance. He was incorrigible, and the truth was the Professor did nothing to rein him in. At moments like these I would raise my hand and say something to the effect of "Three is an important number in philosophy. Nietzsche knows this, and what's more, Nietzsche knows his reader would know this, too. Three is often the number philosophers use to describe the parts of something. Plato says the human soul is divided into three parts. Come to think of it, so does Freud, though you wouldn't catch him using the word *soul*, I suppose. Not only that, there's the Christians, perhaps most important of all, historically at least: the Father, the Son, and the Holy Spirit. So if three is so important in all these instances, it should be as important for stories, or, rather, anecdotes, relating to the individual person. Perhaps Nietzsche is trying to get us to think about the relationship between things and the number three." I did not say this because I believed it, or knew of what I was speaking—I had barely remembered a word of Plato, or Freud, even then, but had heard enough people speak of them so as to say something convincing regarding the two. I said this because it was only through interruption that one could get Roger to cease speaking. Once I had finished stating my rebuttal to him, the Professor smiled slightly—a facial rarity, for him—as if to suggest that in this spat, I had offered the Professor his decisive advantage over Roger, who was, at that moment, questioning the Professor's choice in aphorism, if not in his pedagogy at large, which, to be true, should have been inquisitionally probed, though in Roger's case for the wrong reasons. By providing some haphazard, shaky explanation, I presented Professor Aleister with the necessary blunt instrument he needed to trounce Roger into a mute. In this way I had become Professor Aleister's star pupil, I would say, by acting as his little partner in the classroom. Not a teacher's pet, no—I never so much as complimented the Professor on anything—but in many ways I was an indirect, silent partner to him when he needed it. For this reason, the Professor had urged, particularly toward the end of my schooling years, that I continue toward the life of an academic philosopher.

If I had wanted to do it, I believe I could have. But I simply had no desire to continue with philosophy. My senior thesis was on Heidegger's *Being and Time*, and in it I argued that the concept of "Being," for Heidegger, carried within it a hidden, religious dimension. I said that a gnostic undercurrent is what allowed for "Being," in the texts of Heidegger, to be "revealed." Whereas the "Time" side of things was much more a human endeavor, and therefore decidedly unholy. Time was, in this sense, sacrilegious. After all: What's the one thing outside of which God exists? I did not actually believe this, nor did I know the true significance of what I was writing, but I knew *it was the kind of thing one could write about Heidegger*, a philosopher in whom, I should add, I had little to no investment. I wrote down such things because I could imagine saying these words out loud to my peers and mentors in philosophy, and that in response they would nod their heads solemnly, each asking me, *sotto voce*, to say more. And like incorrigible Roger, I did: my thesis was roughly eighty pages, written, if one can believe it, in a single day, in a single sitting. It was more or less drivel, with a list of secondary sources far below the basic requirements expected for the assignment, and in fact, most of those secondary sources were completely falsified. I made up the names of papers, essays, lectures, books, and authors who had supposedly written on Heidegger. I fabricated an entire literature on the wretched nonsense written by Heidegger, and not one of my superiors, who were all supposed to carefully read and grade this thesis of mine, noticed. I quoted much from William Shrig's study on Heidegger's Gnosticism, titled "Forever Towards Unbeing: Heideggerian Gnosis and the Sacred"—the finer points of this study were invaluable, I suggested. Yes, and I also referenced Sally Zgneiw's "Against the Current: The Baltic Sea as Heidegger's Topos," for its *incredible insight* that the Baltic Sea was the most Heideggerian place on earth, and not the Black Forest, as so many dimwitted scholars had mistakenly believed. And, of course, how could I forget John Jameson Brunk's "The Growing Totality: Heideggerian Time Contra Infinity" for its daring suggestion that Heidegger had been the first person to invent a new concept of time *since the invention of infinity*. My discussion of the above three sources had taken up a good half of my paper, so useful were they to my study and researches. And I had made them all up. None of them existed. I was very high on amphetamines. A drug I no longer take due to my minor heart scare—a heart scare that should not have happened given my age. Not only did I pass, but I received a commendation on my work. Writing that thesis, as I did in the span of an amphetamineabetted sixteen hours, was the equivalent of visiting the purgatory of my mind, effortlessly cranking out pages of nonsense about Heidegger and *Being and Time*, a book that I did in fact read the entire way through, and of which I retained nothing except for a passage that has always stayed with me. In a small, passing moment in the text—practically a footnote—Heidegger recalls Kant's claim that it is the scandal of philosophy that no one has yet proven the existence of the exterior world, of, that is, reality. Heidegger responds that it is the scandal of philosophy that anyone would feel the need to ask this question in the first place. That is, that the world was so self-evidently real, that to be a thinking thing one must, by definition, be inside a world, and that it is philosophers who go about asking absurd questions such as this and waste everyone's time by doing so. The remark seemed true enough to me, and in fact, is probably the only useful insight in the entire book. Heidegger could have stopped writing the book at that moment, and excised everything he had written before it. Then he would have published a book that was the length of a paragraph, a book that would have actually been useful to people, that people would have actually read, and that people could actually understand. Instead he wrote a string of doggerel that, according to his detractors, somehow makes more sense in translation than it does in the original language it was written in: *You just lose something in the original!* they say. I'm no speaker of German, but it isn't hard to believe. Philosophers as a whole function like this—writing careless pablum because one can, because one has earned the degree or station in life to allow oneself to say things like, *Oh, you know, no one has ever really thought about "being" before, have they? Before I started writing this fucking book on being, and—get this—time! Give me a big fucking prize! Give me a grant and a tortured affair with my graduate assistant!*

Yes, it was in my final undergraduate years of study that I stopped experiencing any joy in the writing of essays that were meant to demonstrate fluency in the language of philosophy, where I had to pretend to understand certain concepts by deploying all sorts of specialized terms and idioms that were by their very nature designed to cover over a profound lack of understanding about the nature of the world. I wrote these essays with a permanent grimace, perfunctorily, as if I were performing some awful, rote task I was asked to complete once more, just to show again that, yes, if need be, I could do it. In response to these academic doldrums, as a diversion,

I began writing short snippets of fabulist narrative that I called "novels." They were but a paragraph long each, but to me, they were as good as novels, or as good as any novel one could imagine. And one could read them much more quickly! The truth is I have never gone on at great length. In the writing of these short prose texts—these *novels*—I sought to make this sort of attitude definitive and physical. For when someone goes on at great length, they in fact have very little to say. However long one goes on, it is inversely proportionate to what one has to say. If one is wont to bloviate, to meander, to linger, to assay for very long, it is because one in fact has almost nothing to say; one is filling in the empty locus of their brain with idle chatter. In my own teaching, for example, I have found that when I am least prepared, when I have not prepared one bit, I'm able to lecture at great length—I fill the entire period with my helter-skelter remarks, jumping from one topic to the next with great ease and relish. But if I were to turn over in my mind what I had just shared with my students once the period had concluded, what useful thing had I put to them, I would have to admit I had told them absolutely nothing. In those cases, in those instances, there is not a single useful thing I shared with them. On the other hand, when I plan fastidiously, when I make sure to share only the very necessary and utterly important with my students, I often find that I am finished speaking after about ten or so minutes, and sometimes even less than that. In those cases, I often have to find something to fill the time, something to help us reach the end of the period, something frivolous and not requiring much attention or thought, for I already shared what was essential with them. I might put on a movie. Or I'll tell them to work on their essays quietly, while I sit before them and pretend to scribble something in my notebook. I wrote several of these paragraph-length novels, all taking place in the country of my ancestors, throughout my graduate schooling, when I was studying "creative writing"—a burgeoning field where they teach one to complete short stories. I did not yet wish to enter the world of work. I required still the shelter of schooling, so in that shelter I remained. But, to be clear, I did this not because I wanted to become a writer: it was merely the easiest possible detour away from life. I often had to provide long samples of creative work for my teachers and peers to evaluate, and so I had to bloviate, to meander, to linger, to assay at the length of say, fifteen to twenty pages—meaningless drivel once more, but this time with descriptions of the weather. All the while, I was writing these paragraph-length novels, which I showed to absolutely no one—never to my teachers or my peers, especially—until I had collected an adequate number of them. To my surprise, I quickly found a small publisher who was interested in my paragraph-length novels that took place in the nation of my ancestors, and as such was published as 57 *Colombian Novels*, as there were fifty-seven of these novels, and they all took place in Colombia, or more specifically, in Bogotá. I remember when my short book was accepted for publication by this small publisher, and how I had made a post about it online, announcing to family and friends that in a few months, I would be releasing my very first book of prose fiction, and how one could pre-order such a book on such-and-such a website, and I remember how I felt, with an intense satisfaction verging on delirium, when I saw that Maria was one of the first people to like the post, even going so far as to leave an encouraging comment saying how excited she was for me, and how she couldn't wait to read my book, which she had just ordered. There it was: Maria waiting in anticipation for something having to do with me, with something that had emerged from my body—my mind and eyes and mouth and fingers. I had flirted with the idea of asking the publishers directly if they had actually received an order request from Maria, or if she had simply written this in response to my post in order to be genial to an old friend, but I thought the better of it. I would have had to defend my query, I felt, and I did not want to place myself in a position where I'd have to offer some explanation as to why I was so curious about this person in particular. Besides, I barely spoke to the publishers anyway, who were housed in a city far away from my own, in the middle of the United States. *57 Colombian Novels* emerged without fanfare—I never did hear from Maria, had she read it; the book itself seemed doomed to a total oblivion from its incipience: the so-called publishers printed the book on cheap computer-grade paper, they had somehow included a number of typos that were not in the manuscript I had delivered to them, and what's more, they often failed to ship the final product to a number of people, old friends and family members who would meekly reach out to me, weeks after the book was released, to tell me they had never received it. The book soon after had gone out of print, and I, along with the rest of the world, promptly forgot about it.

As with philosophy, I soon graduated out of the writing of prose fiction. I became an adjunct instructor of first-year composition—freshman essay writing—which is to say, a first-order, badly paid mercenary for the university system. These classes paid so poorly that I had to teach as many of them as I could manage, all but eliminating even the slightest possibility that I would have time to write anything of my own, had I wanted to. Furthermore, I was employed to teach a course that none of my students wanted to take, but which they were required to pass, in the hope, the university would argue, that these same students would receive a *well-rounded liberal arts education*. This was of course a lie. The university system would just as easily do away with as much of the humanities as it could, as they were but leeches on their money-making enterprises—their sole interest—such as their business departments and nursing programs and law schools and the like. The university posited that classes such as the kind I taught, a class whose implicit assumption was that teenagers should know how to put words in a certain order, were necessary if one were to become successful in life, and while they were in this regard correct, or more correct than not, it was not because they were invested in any particular outcome with respect to those students. The university merely needed to present this story to justify its existence. It was obvious to everyone that the story of a *well-rounded liberal arts education* was just another pretext to take more money out of their future pockets. It was obvious to me, it was obvious to my bosses, and most of all, it was obvious to my students. I would feel badly for them, if I were not currently in the position in which they would find themselves in a few short years: as I was selecting my clothes for the evening, after taking a shower and having sat on my bed with my bath towel wrapped around my bottom for the better part of an hour, dreaming away my time as I had been, I decided to check my student loan balance, as I hadn't made a payment in several months, and could see that I presently owed close to twice my annual salary in loans, a large sum of which was money paid toward the interest the bank collected—its profit on my education. It struck me as a great horror, though a horror, of course, tinged with a bathetic comedy, that I was employed in the service of young men and women who had taken out large loans to sit in front of me, and with the little money I received for this work, I would in turn pay my creditors for having had the same experience many years prior. It was for that reason I stopped paying my loans completely—I could not bear it. I had stopped paying my student loans and I had stopped being a writer of short prose fiction. Instead, I performed my health exercises at the academy, then returned home to sit in a chair, drink several domestic beers, and watch videos of men who provided me instructions on ways I could and should improve my life.

There were videos featuring health personages who had advice as to how much protein or carbohydrates one should consume, and there were also videos of men who claimed that taking very brief, cold showers improved them, and other videos that said that eating only according to the dictums of a limited, typically meat-centered diet was the key to one's salvation, while there were others who forbade self-gratification, yet more who said that taking rather small doses of certain psychoactive drugs could help one move beyond the stultifying sleepwalking of contemporary life. And in the comments to all these videos were several young men who claimed their lives were saved because they no longer ate bread, or no longer came to pornography, or no longer cooked eggs in vegetable oils, but in butter: a whole ecosystem of young men who said that they had been saved, very thankfully saved, because they took the advice a man in a video had given them. And the men in these videos were very convincing! And they would, indeed, compete with one another for their salvic purchase in the minds of these many young supplicating men: for example, when I began committing myself to health exercises, I realized early on I required direction for which *kinds* of exercises to perform, how many, for what duration, and so on. To my surprise, there existed an entire cottage industry of videos made expressly for this purpose. And what's more, the personages in these videos even took to commenting on videos others had made within this same arena. One video, for example, would state that performing *face pulls*—where one pulls a weighted rope behind one's head—were the very best exercise for stimulating the anterior deltoids. There was nothing, according to this exercise personage, that was better for one's anterior deltoids than face pulls. What's more: anyone who would suggest otherwise was a complete idiot. And so, of course, there was opposition. As soon as one of these video personages would upload something about how "X was best for Y," another competing video athlete would compose a response that would aim, as best as it could, to not only discredit the advice of that first video, but to humiliate completely its author. They would often suggest this person was hiding something: they were on steroids, of course—just look at them—or they used fake prop weights in their videos, instead of real barbells, or they were promoting some faulty product with false promises of increased testosterone. This attitude generated an entire life-world of rancor and combativeness among the men (they were entirely men) who made these videos—choosing sides, leaving foul comments about so-and-so. I would find myself doing face pulls because I had trusted that original video personage, but then seeing them so thoroughly dishonored, I would cease doing these exercises, following the new program offered by his competitor, assuming they knew all the better what was best for my deltoids—front, side, and anterior—which I was told was the key to giving one the appearance of a man who committed himself to health exercises. I would often waver from one video personage to another—always believing I was then following the very best advice, and indeed, after several years, I had likely found myself in the same position had I merely followed the first: because I had lifted some heavy objects and then put them down again, I was larger, better. My body the product of, as they say, time, strength, cash, and patience!

I closed the web browsing application for my student loan debt and switched to a social media application, one that focused on the writing of short, text-based posts. This social media account was dedicated to my writing of ribald, obscene, incomprehensible fragments—I had made it anonymously, and it did not bear any trace of my name or image—and for some reason or another, several thousand people followed it. I would post something such as "shitting piss/cummm out of my dickkk" and several thousand people would click a button on the user interface to indicate they had enjoyed what it was I had said. I would post something completely fabricated and senseless such as "it's catholic canon that in the garden of gethsemane jesus christ saw every sin committed by human beings which means that he watched a guy blasting rope to waluigi hentai and still decided to sacrifice himself for humanity. absolute legend" and hundreds of thousands of people would congratulate me for having the thought. When this account of mine had first become popular, I felt the rush of fame, albeit for an anonymous avatar, and while no one knew anything about my having to do with it, this did not matter. It felt like an important success, despite the fact that the material I created for this account was intentionally the dumbest and most asinine language I had devised in my entire short life. Soon enough, that initial rush faded, and it became yet another endeavor to which I persisted out of a vague sense of duty. My most recent post had received several hundred likes. I had six new messages, each of them from what seemed like either robots or non-English-speaking accounts, asking me to invest in the newest digital currency Ponzi scheme. I closed the application and opened another, one dedicated to the posting of images. I glumly scrolled through a barrage of posts from people I either barely knew or with whom I had stopped speaking several years prior. Many of these images resembled one another. A woman I had met once at a Marx reading group posted something regarding a local social cause in

Philadelphia that was important to her, it seemed, and in her post, she included information about how you, the viewer of this post, could help with the issue at hand by donating money through a mutual-aid website. Another post from a former high school classmate showcased him and his brother at a baseball game, both of their faces flushed red from, I would imagine, a small deluge of domestic beer. And then I saw Maria had posted something—a picture of herself. This was again continuing her trend: no longer were there pictures of herself with her now ex-husband, of course, nor were there pictures of herself with her dog, or of some new bicycle-racing ephemera, but of her alone. The caption under the post was regarding the forthcoming evening, as it said "New Year's Eve" with a face icon whose eyes looked agog, and whose tongue was jutting out lackadaisically, as if it were drunk. In the image she stood in front of her parents' dirty bathroom mirror, a bathroom mirror I had recognized from pictures she had taken of herself years ago. She wore a gossamer, hot-pink mesh top, one I had seen before, in other photos, though she always wore a black sports bra or some other covering underneath it. This time it was the hot-pink top and nothing else. I could see the full outline of her breasts and even her nipples, which was the first time I had seen them in my life, along with, I presumed, anyone else looking at the photo who had not shared an intimate, nude moment with Maria. The shock of this image was so great that at first it did not strike me as particularly notable. For a moment, it felt as if my brain experienced a delay, the same sort of delay between a live televised broadcast and what appears on a viewer's screen. Once it dawned on me that I was looking at Maria half naked, I felt a shift inside myself I had felt only during very brief, ecstatic moments of sensual pleasure in my life. It was as if the full, sprouted matrix of my consciousness was gathered into a single point—a total penumbral eclipse of my mind, where the whole of my being was reduced to a moment of agape wonder. She looked unbelievable. I felt myself made stupid by an overwhelming lust and double tapped my thumb on my phone screen to indicate that I had liked the post. I had done this without thinking, as if my body had proceeded without my consent. This was all to my severe chagrin: she had posted the image a mere twenty-five seconds prior to my liking it, and I was clearly the first person to have done so, almost immediately after she had posted it. Anyone else in the world gazing upon her account from their device—whether they be in Tasmania or Norway or Jamaica—could see that I, of all people on the planet, had been the first person to like an image of Maria where her breasts were entirely visible. I shut off my phone. A devastating wave of shame swept over me, and I felt that, at this very early stage in my evening, I had already committed an error that I could not fix. I turned my phone on again and returned to Maria's profile. I thought of messaging her: *Yo! You coming to the Professor's house tn?* I would write, *can't wait to catch up !! xoxo.* I typed out this message on my phone, deleted it, tried a different variation, and deleted that one, too. I looked again at her post and saw that forty-eight people had liked it in the intervening five minutes or so since I had done the same. Most of these accounts belonged to women, it seemed, though it was difficult to tell from some of the animated avatar photographs these users had chosen for their accounts, as well as the usernames they had selected, for example, "forestationwhore69." I recognized a few: her sister, a friend from our university days with whom Maria often spent time, though I never knew her well. I saw, too, that some men had liked the photograph. The only one I recognized: Roger. I felt myself clench. What a fucking idiot! What a dog. A clown. He barely knew her. I had not once seen them speak with each other during our schooling days, and more than once I had heard Maria directly mock him. In that same Nietzsche class, I remember, when Roger would go on with the Professor, I would notice that Maria, who in that class always sat to my left, would often tap her leg irritably, moving it up and down in a quick, agitated motion, occasionally glancing at the clock above the chalkboard, waiting for this chronic tête-a-tête between Roger and the Professor to cease, and for the class to be dismissed early, as it always was. And I remember that, without thinking, without so much as premeditating, I reached my hand out and placed it on her thigh, squeezing it gently, and whispered, "Relax, Maria, it's almost over," and how surprised she looked, seeing that I had touched her like that—as I had never touched her—and how she looked back at me and smiled, then just as quickly made a face, almost jeeringly, as if to say back to me, "Oh, you, knock it off." And I remember that she chuckled—she looked chuffed—and said, "Sorry if I'm being annoying," presuming, it seemed, that her foot tapping had irritated me. I was so overwhelmed from this light touch, I recall, that I felt my heart accelerate as if it were injected directly with adrenaline, and I could barely manage a fake laugh in response to her apology, suggesting that it really wasn't such a big deal, hiding as best as I could how massively this small touch had affected me. I felt I had climbed some unforeseen peak of the possibility of desire itself, though as for Maria, she seemed to have forgotten the moment instantly, for I remember she closed her copy of *Ecce Homo* and opened a notebook, whereupon she jotted down items to acquire at the grocer: "Turnips, ice cream, paper towels," it said. Maria was always writing lists like these; chores she needed to tend to, assignments she needed to complete. She would later tell me that list-making was the secret to life itself, that she could not get a single thing done if she had not sat down and written it first in her notebook. She encouraged me to do the same, and I took her up on it: since my university days, I had become an inveterate maker of lists: books to read, concepts to consider, behaviors to change.

In fact, I had been jotting down such a list in the past December weeks. It is impossible for me to approach a new year without creating an inventory for what I wish to accomplish in the next. For several years, I have been in the habit of drafting a massive list—a master list of life—that one may call "New Year's resolutions." Often, I've heard these resolutions are de facto acts of bad faith: if one wanted to change something in their habits or behavior, in how they comported themselves in their day-to-day living, one should do so immediately, without hesitation. If one is in the habit of saying, "Tomorrow, I will," one might as well say, "Tomorrow, I won't," or "Tomorrow, I will, but the day after, I won't," for resolutions are things to be taken immediately, in the present moment, when one can exercise imminent control. One has no control of what emerges in the future, and the same of course can be said for what has already passed: a truth verging on the bromidic. So, a New Year's resolution in this sense can only be taken as the worst form of this weak, mental plea. One doesn't want to actually speak French when they write "Learn French" on their resolution list—they want to be the sort of person who *already speaks French*. But on this head, I can say with certainty that I am at odds with the average fellow. And it's because of this I've taken to drafting New Year's resolutions every year: I actually do what I set out for myself. I complete my tasks! No, I do not learn French, nor will I ever, God permitting. But by every December, I've crossed each item off my list. I have not failed once. Every year I put to myself a number of tasks and a single, behavioral intention. This past year, for instance, one of these New Year's resolutions was to learn calculus. I had always hated math in my schooling years—I avoided it at all costs—and therefore felt the need to prove to myself, now as an adult, that my character had fundamentally transformed. I achieved this by sitting down for a period of some months and taught myself a subject often considered difficult for the student of mathematics. I purchased textbooks on the subject, and watched a variety of tutorials on how to go about the learning of such a thing. I spent hours banging my head against my textbooks, quite literally. I experienced such spasms of frustration that I would often raise my textbooks above my head and smash them upon my forehead as hard as I could muster. I felt that if my inability to master my subject had to be reprimanded with a bout of self-flagellation, I could raise the material stakes of my resolution: either I learned calculus, or I would give myself brain damage. I was successful with the former—as for the latter, who is to say. Yes, every year I seek to disturb my inner climate for the better: to change that weather to accommodate an even more capacious sensibility. I was now, having completed my previous year's resolutions quite successfully, in the position to draft new items for my list. As Charles Lamb put it, "No one regards the first of January with indifference." The trouble was that while in previous years I was always able to come up with a list that was, if anything, *too* ambitious, this year, it seemed I was coming up dry. Every day, I make a list for myself of things I must attend to, and almost every one of those days, this list far exceeds what it is possible to accomplish in the sixteen or so waking hours each of us is allotted in the human day. Once, however, due to my diligence and quick action, I did in fact cross each item off my list, and what's more, before dinnertime. I had nothing else I needed to accomplish, and it struck me like a horror: to have no more items to cross off a list was worse, it seemed, than to have failed utterly in having accomplished the most basic duties of one's day. It seemed to me now that I was in somewhat a similar position as I had been that day, except for my entire, forthcoming year.

While selecting my clothes for the evening, having air-dried for the better part of an hour, sitting on the lip of my bed as I had been, staring at the blank wall before me in my studio apartment, I thought that perhaps it was time to become a man who took to clothing himself with greater show and elegance. For the majority of my adult life, I'd grown accustomed to wearing the equivalent of a cartoon character's wardrobe: every day I donned a simple button-down shirt, typically of the Oxford variant, and a pair of light-wash denim jeans. I wore this to work and everywhere else I needed to go that wasn't work. The sole place—the only place—I did not wear this combination was at the gymnasium, as it was not the appropriate uniform for my body academy. There I resorted to a plain shirt and fleece shorts. Just as soon as I'd reenter the gymnasium locker room, however, I'd go back to my trusted Oxford button-down shirt and light-wash denim jeans. I often fell asleep in these clothes. So as I was slowly putting on my boxer briefs and brightly colored socks (my sole sartorial indulgence), I thought that perhaps I could allow some greater variation in my life in the manner of my clothing. But no, whether this be in my future or not, buying new clothes was not material fit for a New Year's resolution list. This list was to me a blueprint—a playbook, as it were—for all that I would come to embody in the following year, and as such I needed to set my aim for something worth the time to come. Unfortunately, it appeared I had already improved myself so much with these previous New Year's resolutions that I had nothing else to do. I put on my favorite navy-blue button-down Gap Oxford, and my most-worn-in Levi's jeans. I checked my phone once more, as well as my social media applications, and noted that well over a hundred people had liked Maria's photo, and at least a dozen had left a comment on her post—fire-image reactions as well as a variety of comments that ranged from "girlllllll" and "MA-RIA" and "babe"—all of which seemed to have been left by close friends, or perhaps people claiming a familiarity with Maria that was impossible to decipher as either authentic or forced.

It was only eight in the evening, but because it had been dark since a little before five, it felt later than it was, as was often the case in North American northeastern winter. Professor Aleister said he would begin expecting guests around seven, and since the trip, including walking from my apartment to the subway, and then switching to the regional rail, and then walking from the train station to the Professor's house, would take a little over an hour, I decided it an appropriate time to finally leave. I checked my appearance in the single mirror I kept in the apartment. I looked like the normal version of myself, which somehow disappointed me. Next to the mirror I had pasted a quotation from Pascal, which I read every time I left my apartment: "All of humanity's problems stem from man's inability to sit quietly in a room alone." I had written this with my own hand, on a random scrap of paper, and pasted it onto the wall with blue painter's tape—I had planned to have the quote printed upon respectable card stock and framed, but always found some greater reason or other for putting off this small task. Besides, my studio basement apartment was sparsely decorated, and I had always maintained it so, for it gave the illusion that the apartment was bigger than it was, and that I would soon move somewhere else. I no longer kept shelves, for instance, and merely scattered my books in piles across the floor. I had removed my kitchen table and its accompanying wooden chair, as it seemed just as easy to sit on the floor when I felt the urge to eat. I employed a cheap card table for a desk, a plastic folding chair for a seat, and these accommodations seemed sufficient enough to me. I had been living in this apartment for six years, for it was let astonishingly cheap: $600 and not a cent further. My landlord never once raised the rent, despite my living in an increasingly expensive neighborhood on the northern border of South Philadelphia, where several new specialty shops and fast casual restaurants cropped up year by year, offering confections such as turkey sandwiches made with a cranberry-miso glaze, which the proprietor of those establishments decided should cost nineteen dollars. Every month I'd walk half a mile to my landlord's apartment and slide a check under his door—checks that would often go uncashed for months at a time, leading me to wonder, then, whether or not he had finally died, as he was quite old. I would fantasize about staying in my apartment unbothered until some young, upwardly mobile couple bought the place, or the city requisitioned it due to unpaid property taxes. Those checks would be cashed eventually, of course, and that fantasy would just as soon be dashed. I looked again at the Pascal quote: Have you sat quietly alone in your room? Must you go out? What pressing matter is there outside that you must attend to? For a full year, I had left my apartment only to go to the gym. Otherwise, I had all my necessities delivered to me. I had seen no one, and I had spoken to no one: I had not said a word out loud in three hundred and sixty-four days, not even to myself. The last person with whom I had shared words was the English department secretary, the previous December, who, as I was checking my faculty mailbox before parting, asked me what I planned to do with my winter break, after my accident. I said that I planned to sit quietly alone in my room and ask myself, Must you go out? What pressing matter is there outside you must attend to? Must you speak? She offered a concerned and secular "Happy holidays" in response, and I bid her goodbye. After nearly a decade of carrying out the misery labor of an adjunct professor, I decided I could no longer return to teaching, and further yet, I could no longer dedicate myself to any profession where it was incumbent upon me to speak. I would no longer be a speaker, and, indeed, my chief resolution for this past year was to take a vow of silence. This seemed to me the best possible New Year's resolution. And the reasons for this had to do with an episode during my final weeks as a teacher, last December: I had, at one university, been given a course on Irish literature—and had to provide a history of the leprechaun. I had, for some reason or other, become obsessed with the leprechaun as a figure. There was something *overly of the leprechaun of it*, it seemed. And I gave a rousing performance for my class. I spoke unabashedly, without script, for a full seventy minutes without pausing for breath once, and it seemed that my students in this class, having gotten used to my downtrodden performances, were so overtaken by the vigor with which I was telling them of the history of the leprechaun that, as the last words of my lecture left my mouth, my students—if it can be believed—applauded me. I had experienced a high so delicious that, as I left the room and boarded a bus to teach my next class at a different university, I was overtaken by the urge to repeat my performance—to regain the high—and so had decided I would deliver the exact same speech I had just provided. Except that, while in the first case, my lecture was to be delivered for a class on the history of Irish literature, my next class was entitled "Multimedia Business Writing 102," and yet I did not allow this to deter me. According to the syllabus, I was to go over citation procedures for this day's lecture, and instead, I tore into my lecture on the leprechaun, the history of the leprechaun, how there was *too much of the leprechaun about it*, of course, and to illustrate by contrast the purported diminutiveness of the leprechaun, I stood on my lectern before my students to deliver the second half off my speech. I pulled a student's chair to help me ascend to the top of the lectern, which was tilted on a slant, and so I had to try my very best to retain my balance as I regaled my students with the history of the leprechaun. And while I was atop my lectern, gazing at my students below, I felt a stricture—a tightness around my chest. On the bus ride over, I remembered how, a few weeks prior, I had found a sole amphetamine capsule in my closet, a leftover from my days of using such a substance which had initially led to my first heart scare. And I had placed this capsule in my wallet, with the idea that, perhaps, someday, when the occasion called for it, I would once again take this amphetamine capsule and relive a little the euphoria it could deliver. So, on the bus, I placed it in my mouth and swallowed it dry. Its effects had of course made my second performance all the more effusive, yet unfortunately, too much so. For as I stood on the lectern, the tightness around my chest grew ever more painful and I was forced to cease my speech. It was then I collapsed. I fell teeth first onto the floor below me, my mouth making direct contact with the marble floor, for when I awoke—the building's security guard stood over me, with my students huddled around in a throng—I discovered that I had in fact lost all of my front teeth, so hard had I hit the floor that they shattered. I had broken my nose as well. At the hospital, the doctor suggested I likely experienced an acute bout of tachycardia due to my large dose of amphetamines, which he said, I should never take again given my heart history. And for this indulgence, I had lost my teeth. I decided then, indeed, I would lose my speech, too, for a year. I had stopped working. I had stopped responding to messages delivered to me. I had not opened my mail; as soon as it was delivered to my doorstep, I would promptly dump the contents into my waste bin. I had used nearly all of my savings to continue to pay for my admittedly modest expenses, and I was almost without money. I did not know what I would do. Though bittersweet, it felt appropriate that I would be unsuccessful with my resolution to not speak for a year: if Maria should be at the Professor's, I had my speeches to deliver. I left my apartment.

Crying

I walked a few blocks up to South Street and turned left, toward Broad. The New Year's revelers were already out, several of them visibly drunk, many screaming and laughing at one another. This was often the scene on South Street on any given weekend, but it was now, despite the cold, at a heightened pitch. Every other young person appeared barely old enough to drink alcohol, though I did not chide them: I was once quite like that, seeking any opportunity to derange my senses with a combination of beer, whatever drugs were readily available, and above all else, cigarettes. Of all the vices I had removed from my life, it was those I missed most—cigarettes had seemed to me the perfect thing to do at any given time. I couldn't envision a moment of life that could not be subtly massaged into a greater sense of aesthetic pleasure with a cigarette. But given my unexpected heart scare, and the deleterious effects cigarettes are known to impart on that most essential muscle, I had to put those lovely sticks on the shelf for good. I no longer missed their presence in my life physically, but a spiritual longing for them persisted, and I did not expect that particular spear of my spirit to go blunted for likely the rest of my life. Like Zeno, I had to write "last cigarette" across the gates of my consciousness, except I actually meant it. Across the street, a few boys wearing bright, garish winter coats were each puffing away at their digital smoking devices—devices I had always found repulsive—and screaming obscenities at one another. One of their number kept saying, "Going to get some Fishtown pussy tonight!" and the others would laugh and tilt their heads down, clapping loudly while running around one another in a short circle. "Taking the El to some Fishtown pussy tonight," the boy repeated, and his comrades continued encouraging him. "Getting that, ah"—he could not contain his laughter—"getting that, ah, fine ass charcuterie board pussy," he said. The place of which they spoke had, for decades, been an Irish working-class neighborhood dedicated to fish mongering—hence the name—but which had, in the last ten years, completely transmogrified through the slow, necrotic disease of gentrification, transforming the dive bars into organic parenting stores and the like. I had once lived there, many years ago, and saw that transformation firsthand. The archetypical Fishtown woman of which this boy spoke was likely one such addition to that neighborhood. "Getting that podcast pussy tonight," the boy said again, and his retinue continued their encouraging hollers. I found their blitheness untoward. I felt the urge to tell them to keep their proposals to themselves—not everyone on South Street needed to hear whom they were planning on bedding by the evening's end. I envisioned myself approaching the group and chastising them for their excessive public display, thereby imparting the seed of good manners. Yes, and having anticipated how these boys would likely cower in response to my interdictions, I felt satisfied enough with my fantasy, and let my irritation subside. I continued forward, heading west, with a slight spring in my gait. But once I had been emptied of that vexation, I felt something move darkly within my thoughts, and indeed irritation transformed into self-rebuke: those were young boys, after all, prone to garrulous displays of masculine, heterosexual libido, and here I was, at least a decade and a half older, essentially performing the very same task as them, guided by the very same hope. I made no fuss about it—I projected no braggadocious intentions—but I was taking an hour-long journey to the Philadelphia suburbs—where I thought I would never, ever return—all for the small chance I might speak with a woman I had not spoken to in years and with whom I was hoping I would wake up to naked the coming morning.

On the remainder of my journey west through South Street, I walked past a neon-lighted sex-toy shop; a Vietnamese soupery which was to my surprise still open; a few bars blaring electronic dance music; and a queue of people lined up for one of Philadelphia's famous steak sandwiches. It was cold, though as I built up a rhythm on my walk, that chill dissipated. My phone said there was a 70 percent chance of snow flurries later in the evening, but the ground would be too warm for it to stick meaningfully. Once on Broad, I descended the subway steps and was, as always, accosted by the smell of overcooked urine and stale, Center City rot. There was already New Year's Eve detritus near the turnstile—empty beer cans, cigarettes butts, bags of chips and candy. I swiped my SEPTA card and to my delight found the train pulling into the station as soon as I emerged onto the platform. Once installed in my seat on the subway to the regional rail, my thoughts returned to Professor Aleister: I had not seen him since graduation, a realization that surprised me, though of course I had known this all along. *Although I am alone and a widower,* his email had said, *I won't let that get in the way of the little time I have left in life.* The Professor, it was true, must now be in his mid- to late eighties; he was already quite old when I was his student, well over a decade ago, and I remember hearing gossip back then that the chair of the Humanities department was keen to find an excuse that would lead Professor Aleister toward what was then a long-overdue retirement. The death of his wife, I imagined, must have been what led to that necessary outcome. But who else from his family would be present this evening? His wife was always curiously absent when we'd visit the Professor's house—whenever Robert or Thomas or Maria would note this, Professor Aleister would say something or other regarding her work, and how it required frequent and extensive travel. The only time I asked what it was she did, he quoted to me a line from a novel. He said, "You get justice in the next world. In this world, you have the law." And she worked for the law, he said, whatever that meant. There was a picture of the two of them displayed in their house, I remember, on what was likely their wedding day: a washed-out photograph where the couple stood in front of what appeared to be the steps of a Roman amphitheater: a much younger version of the Professor in crumpled, festive garb, and his young wife with long, dark hair, elegant and equally festive, though she carried her face like someone who was quite tired. The other personal photograph I remembered was of their son as a child of about six or seven, who by now must be well into his fifties. Professor Aleister, when discussing his sole child, only had pejorative remarks reserved for him—complaints about the social and financial troubles in which his son, Albert, had always found himself. He had dealt with both a drug and gambling problem, it seemed (the Professor never said so outright), and I surmised that the Professor had been estranged from Albert for some years. During these speaking sessions at the Professor's house—where all manner of topics were permitted, so he said—his family life was the only subject that was strictly verboten: when one spoke about such family matters—whether related to oneself or to the Professor's—he would pretend he hadn't heard a word of what had been said, and just as quickly move on to the next, more pressing philosophic or literary issue at hand.

Our occasional correspondence in the last few years carried that very same spirit, for the Professor and I would discuss only what had lightly bonded us in the first place: our shared love of literature, and of collecting out-of-print editions of obscure and little-known books. Our mutual bibliophilism was sufficient grounds to lubricate our relationship after I had ceased being his student. At school, I would often stop by his office to discuss the forthcoming releases from presses such as New Directions or Dalkey Archive—the publication of important international books that were being introduced to the English-reading public for the first time. And so our emails essentially maintained the shape of these brief office visits. He would email me about some unknown, underread Italian writer and I would in turn respond with a Japanese writer I had recently discovered whom he might like. In response, the Professor would report news of a new translation from the Hungarian, of an oft-overlooked novelist who committed suicide quite young, and I would parry that with information on, say, the forthcoming English-language release of a seminal though rather obscure Surrealist text, and the Professor would say he had already read it in its original French. I would then say that if he had enjoyed such a book, he should read Camelia Chittle and, of course, Jacques Vaché. And he would then say I should read Félicien Marboeuf, as well as Jurgen Hollar, author of *Any Trick to Finding*, a book, I would then admit to him, I myself had already read and actually thought of as rather underwhelming. And that really, who he should be reading is Oren Mabb, author of *Boats I Deserve*, a sui generis science fiction poem I described as if Anton Platonov had developed rabies that had fully matured in his brain and began writing poems like Robert Desnos, or even, if you'll allow it, Hannah Weiner, though in the single interview Mabb granted, he said the only writer he had ever admired was Comte de Lautréamont, that in fact he had learned French in order to read *Maldoror* in its original, and as soon as he had read it in its original once, he had never read it again, nor did he have a single thought in French, ever again. Mabb had said that, after reading *Maldoror*, unlearning French was the greatest pleasure in his life. Like with conversations at his house, emails between the Professor and me rarely touched on personal matters, though he did occasionally invite me over—*like when you were under my tutelage*, he'd say—but I would always find some reason to avoid meeting him there. He would often bribe me with the promise of books and alcohol: *You must come over*, he'd say in one of these emails, *I've just found a Spanish first edition of Schwob's* Imaginary Lives, *and I recently acquired a bottle of Midleton, vintage 2013, that you must try*, he'd say. I would always be busy whatever the date, or range of dates, he would provide me. I always had some pressing matter or appointment that evening, I'd say, that I could not manage to put off. I had to wash my hair. The more I rebuffed his offers, the less frequently he'd suggest them, though they would continue to drip into my inbox on occasion. This invitation to his New Year's Eve party was perhaps the first time I had been invited over to his house in about a year and a half, and as I had RSVP'd only a few hours before leaving my apartment, I did not hear

· 77 ·

back from him. I wondered, as I switched over from the subway to the regional rail, if he was excited to see me. My reasons for refusing his invitations were obscure even to me; I enjoyed sharing book recommendations, it was true, and had discovered quite a few more obscure writers due to the Professor's large and omnivorous life of reading, writers and poets such as Angus Onions III and Jean-Pierre Brisset, whom I would later read approvingly. I had supposed, to some degree, I wished to keep the Professor's influence over my life to a minimum. Our camaraderie over books and literature was enough, and I wished to sequester anything beyond that in the foregone past. He, after all, had his little assistant to play with: young Max, a recent graduate from our alma mater, whom I was made aware had become, after his graduation, employed as a research-assistant-cum-secretary for the Professor. I discovered this through Professor Aleister's active social media profile. The Professor used an older one of these services—a social media site once very popular, though which now had fallen into disuse outside of a decidedly older user base, who had naturally come to it late in its lifecycle. I maintained my account on it as a way to keep track of the few people, such as Professor Aleister, who continued to use it. On it, he'd often post short essays—two or three paragraphs—on some fragment from Lichtenberg, for example, or his thoughts on a new movie he had just seen, but as more often was the case, he would post a blurry, out-of-focus photograph of his personal assistant, young Max, and an extract from a conversation they had just reportedly held. Why Professor Aleister needed a personal assistant was puzzling—he had not published many translations over the last several years, though he would often post, say, about some new book he had acquired in the Catalan which had piqued his interest. Still, whatever half-hearted translation project he might suggest was afoot in his life, I found it difficult to imagine this would require so much work he would need to call upon the administrative help of a young man. My assumption was that the Professor offered Max a paid position as his assistant mostly as an excuse to have someone around for him to talk to all day, perhaps as a temporary social bulwark against the loneliness of retirement, and, as I had recently discovered, widowhood. To some degree, I imagined, the Professor had developed a remora-like relationship to the young, a necessity to be around men and women in their twenties to whom he could impart a few words of advice, regardless of whether or not those words had any effect. This growing realization throughout the course of my relationship with Professor Aleister had spawned a sense of resentment in me—often when those emails from the Professor had arrived in my inbox, I'd notice that he would barely remark on anything I had said in my previous message, almost outright ignoring my own remarks, observations, or questions, in favor of detailing some new scheme, comment, or idea he had been occupied with in the past weeks. Even as an old man, it seemed, he felt the need to be admired as some object of intellectual devotion, and required a permanent audience to attest to that identity. In some of these emails he'd let slip a memory of how he had, for example, been a guest judge in some translation contest of sorts, or how he had rejected a particular prize or commendation from some cultural institute, because he deemed it below him. *There was that time, back in the nineties, I was invited down to Mexico City*, he'd say, *they wanted to fête me. But I declined. I need not be fêted!*

The train approached its destination. It had been some years since I made my way to these suburbs,

suburbs where I myself had lived and studied while I was a student. As the train passed familiar shops, the memories of those nights returned to me. Many nights of quiet reading and conversation with Robert, Thomas, and Maria, though just as many nights spent in a stupor, drunk and smoking a joint in some corner of a suburban forest, whereupon one (or all) of us would vomit the contents of our stomach on a poor, undeserving pine tree. Despite our forceful and far-reaching debauchery, we were never once reprimanded by a university authority, and once we were old enough to drink legally, we became that much more audacious in our merrymaking, openly drinking forty ounces of malt liquor in our dormitory hallways: Olde English, St. Ides, or—if we were feeling particularly wretched—Hurricane High Gravity, which had an ABV over 8 percent. Maria spent one semester of her junior year abroad in Paris, I remember, and upon returning, she turned her nose up at the malt liquor we were all so acquainted with drinking, because it was so cheap. Paris had changed her! Now she drank only wine. I recalled, then, a quote from John Ashbery that Maria had shared with me, when she returned: "After you've lived in Paris for a while, you don't want to live anywhere, including Paris." After her Parisian episode, Maria had become obsessed with anything French, and especially its literature. On the final night the four of us visited Professor Aleister's house, I remember, she had worn a red dress with black shoes: just like the Duchesse de Guermantes, she said, in—what I didn't know then, as I had not yet read it—my favorite scene from all of Proust, when poor Charles tells the Duchesse he's soon to die, and the Duc de Guermantes, only listening with half an ear, chastises his wife for her sartorial choices, forcing her to go inside and change. (Was it my favorite scene because it was Maria's favorite, as well?) At that final meeting at the Professor's, we all decided to play a game: we would show up, as a send-off to the Professor and to our time as his students, in our best finery. Robert and Thomas wore black tie, three-piece suits, Maria was regaled in her Guermantes best, but I—always ready with the ulterior interpretation—took this injunction toward finery (it was Maria's idea) as a chance to wear a costume: I arrived wearing a buckskin coat, bolo tie, and red kerchief across my neck. And alligator boots. This they all found rather funny and mercilessly teased me, especially Maria—my outfit had literally brought her to tears—though I did not find it so funny. Surely these clothes represented finery to someone! The Professor was unamused by our game, as he did not so much as deign to mention our choice in clothing, had he even noticed it. That final meeting went very much like all the others, and I could sense a certain crestfallenness among us, perhaps having anticipated some sort of crescendo to punctuate all those many meetings at the Professor's. I remember us late that evening walking back to our campus lodgings silently, interrupted at last by Maria, who said: *Well, I think we all look very fetching, at least.* I wished then someone had taken a picture of us, of Maria in her red dress, and me in my cowboy costume, and I said aloud, "I wish we had a picture of us," and Robert and Thomas were silent once more, but Maria, after a long pause, allowed: "Well, isn't that nice." I had wondered how long it had been since she had spoken with the Professor. As far as I knew from my own brief missives with Professor Aleister, they didn't maintain a correspondence, or at the very least, he never mentioned it. Indeed, if Maria had graduated out of philosophy as she said—if she had decisively left it behind, now that she continued into real life—I couldn't imagine why she would want to spend her evening alongside him

once more. The Professor would not offer the cour-
tesy of small chatter—*How have you been? Where are
you working now?*—he would jump straight into the
only topics that he deemed appropriate for discussion under his roof. Maybe, if I were sly enough, I
would be able to cut my time down at the Professor's
house to a concise half hour, so easy would it be to
convince Maria to spend the remainder of her New
Year's Eve with me at Dirty Frank's or maybe even
El Bar in Fishtown—where we could really catch up,
away from the Professor's octogenarian prattle.

The walk from the train station to the Professor's house was straightforward and perfunctory.
All suburban walking is debased, shameful: a distance of a mile in the suburbs can feel as if one
were walking through some expensive, inhospita-
ble desert—at any moment some terrible buzzard
might swoop down and pluck you up. This meta-
phorical buzzard would, in the case of the suburbs,
take the form of a family-size SUV driving homi-
cidally down the street, ready to murder you for
the trespass of daring to walk where there are no
sidewalks, because they didn't bother to build them
in the first place. A mile walk in the city is, on the
other hand, a kind of dream—one forgets how long

one has been walking, so accosted has one been by lights and myriad other machine sounds, overheard conversations, and other plasticine images. So while Philadelphia was bustling, it appeared as if its suburbs had already gone to sleep, not anywhere close to midnight. Perhaps its people had no use for the pageantry, or indeed for the concept of New Year's Eve entirely. Their fate had already been decided for them, and they were happy to merely repeat the same thing they had done the year prior, ad infinitum, ad nauseam, until their deaths. I walked past a few houses with their lights on, and massive flat-screen televisions clearly visible through their Victorian bay windows. One such instance of this was so arresting that I found myself stopped in front of the house, gazing into the family den. Four middle-aged-to-elderly men sat in plush recliners with the footstool sprung before them, all watching a movie which, at the moment I caught a glimpse of it, prominently displayed the breasts of what looked like a familiar actress. What's more, the very next scene continued the theme of what it had just shown, for a second woman—who might herself have been a famous actress—also appeared totally in the nude, apparently cavorting with the first woman in a manner that resembled the kinds of actions one initiates before sexual intercourse. Just then, a nude man appeared—stroking a full erection—apparently watching the two women, ready to enter into the fray himself. What followed was pornographic, and it dawned on me then that this was a pornographic film that had been made to resemble a famous movie; perhaps it was, in this sense, a spoof of its legitimate Hollywood counterpart. I felt then that I myself was watching a movie of my own: a movie about four elderly men watching a pornographic parody of a famous film, seated together silently on New Year's Eve—who unknowingly had a man of thirty-five years, seventy inches, slender make, and a mouth full of dental veneers stand before their house in a desolate suburban street. It was only when my own appearance was reflected back at me in their bay window by the lights of a passing car, steam billowing from my nostrils, the tip of my nose far gone into redness and slightly numb, was I jolted from this scene and hurried away, fearing I had done something awful, but not being able to place what it was I had done. I was presently only five minutes away from the Professor's house, and already the familiarity of my surroundings was returning to me, though the images of these suburban streets had always been slightly inchoate, as I was often under the influence while walking toward, and especially away from, the Professor's house all those years in the past. It then occurred to me that I *had* indeed committed a terrible error: I brought with me nothing. No customary bottle of wine, no homemade treat, nor even a humble six-pack of beer. While I assumed there would be plenty of refreshments at the party, it was indecorous of me to stride up to the door completely empty-handed. I thought, briefly, of turning toward the main road in town—I recalled the general direction—and finding a late-night shop that at the very least sold beer I could bring with me. By my calculations, however, the walk there and back would add forty-five minutes to my journey and could potentially risk my joining in the celebratory throng past an ideal point—Maria might already be in the doorway, putting on her scarf and thanking the Professor for having her this evening, but claiming that she needed to return to her parents' home before it got too late. She'd see me entering the Professor's house and grasp my arm gently and say she was so sorry to have missed me, but she was glad that she could at least say a brief hello and goodbye before she was off. I decided against it.

The Professor's house appeared to me the same as ever. A typical early twentieth-century colonial with garish vinyl siding and a completely ornamental chimney off to one side. Curiously, there weren't any cars in the driveway—I had imagined that a fair number of the party would be driving, out in the suburbs as this gathering was, and that the driveway would be crammed with sedans and trucks extending out onto the street. The lights on the first floor were on, but not above it. Even more strange, I could not catch even a silhouette of a partygoer through the sheer-curtained windows. I ascended the few stone steps of the Professor's house and rang the doorbell. I stood silently for close to a minute, and not having been greeted by either the Professor or another partygoer, nor hearing anything stirring within the house, I rang again, pressing the buzzer several times for emphasis, which at first felt excessive and childlike, but then just as quickly well-earned: I understood why one would want to announce their arrival so forcefully—I had sojourned here with purpose! I needed to prepare the various lines and small speeches I'd give:

a knowing, recondite greeting to the Professor, a more jovial if not almost ribald repartee with Robert and Thomas, and finally a slightly taken-aback-if-not-entirely-bowled-over embrace with Maria, as if to say to her: How much I've missed you; oh, how much you've been on my mind; how much have I been waiting for an opportunity just like this one. Having waited another minute in silence, I tried my luck with the door, and discovered it had been unlocked all this while. I stepped inside the Professor's welcoming den—a sunroom of sorts, though at this hour it was shrouded in darkness. It, like the outside, appeared to me much the same as it had years ago: a wrought-iron table with garden chairs tucked away in the corner, the table itself covered in unopened envelopes and other mail garbage. Next to the table was a floor-to-ceiling bookshelf filled with oversize hardbacks—art books and cookbooks and so on—and, as was the case in my previous visits, there were several potted plants along the walls and large windows: pothos, dumb cane, philodendron, and a few succulents. While the pots and their respective plants remained in their expected places, once my eyes had adjusted to the darkness, I could see all the plants in this sunroom were decayed and long dead. Even those cacti, the consummate lazy man's plant, were desiccated into gourd-like debasements of themselves. Dried, withered leaves littered the ground all over, and they crunched underneath me as I walked over them. An image foolishly came to me: I am the released captive, returning to Plato's cave. I made my way through another door that opened into the Professor's living room and farther down, his dining room, where we'd so often gather for one of his speaking sessions. Like the den before it, the living room floor was also littered with materials—books stacked halfway to the ceiling, loose sheaves of paper, plastic bags with long CVS receipts inside them, empty takeout containers, cardboard boxes filled with heteroclite junk, and so forth. At the far end of the dining room sat Professor Aleister, alone, staring directly at me. There were no other people.

I stood in his dirty living room, gazing back at him. The Professor looked awful. He was so thin it seemed like his skeleton were pushing itself out from the inside of his body. His beard—which he had never fashioned before ("one must earn their beard," he often said)—was long, tangled, and uneven. He wore a beige cardigan that was discolored throughout. The arms of his thin, rectangular glasses splayed outwardly from his face in opposite diagonal directions. The Professor appeared alert, as if he were awaiting an assailant, ready to deal with them as they came. It was an expression, if I recalled correctly, that he used with all of his students.

"There's beer in the fridge," the Professor said, as I approached. "Mind the books."

I walked into the kitchen behind him. It was in as sorry a shape as the living and dining room, though emptier, which gave its dirtiness a less offensive character. I opened the refrigerator door, and the fridge was filled with books. I opened his freezer, and saw that it, too, was filled with books—titles in French and Spanish and Catalan, many of which I didn't recognize. In the fridge were five beers and a plastic container of milk that was mostly full. According to its label, it had expired three weeks prior. I grabbed a beer and made my way back to the dining room, where I removed some papers from the surface of a chair and placed them on the dining room table. It was littered with all sorts of reading material: critical books on philosophy, various monographs, biographies, detective novels. I brought my newly uncluttered chair closer to the Professor, and sat opposite him. I did not take off my coat.

"Many years ago," the Professor said, "I read a book by a Chilean who wrote about a man living in Mexico, and the man has gone completely insane. He begins hanging books on the clothesline outside, books of geometry, if I recall, to expose the concepts within those books to the elements, as it were. I have no clothesline, so I put the books in the fridge. If what they say is true, they shouldn't mind the cold too much. They should prove themselves against it, in fact. If the concepts within those books are solid, if they are sound, they should not care in the least about the artificial cold of my icebox. I should have done this years ago," he said, and broke off abruptly. We sat in silence. I looked around the room for something, but there wasn't anything.

"Concepts need to prove themselves against other concepts," he said. "It's true, and other arguments and appraisals and perspectives. And they must prove themselves against the world they inhabit even more so, which involves the cold, the shit, the piss, a fire, illness, whatever. I've always maintained that a philosopher is a writer of prose texts who uses concepts much the same way a novelist uses characters. Both are fictions that aim to generate some kind of mental effect on the reader of them. When one thinks of Don Quixote, one imagines a frail, deluded man—a man ruined by his reading, like so many of us. If Cervantes was a philosopher, and not a writer of the first great novel, he would not have written *Don Quixote*, but the Don Quixote concept. Kant invented the concept of the categorical imperative, but had he been a writer of fiction from his age, say, like the writer Jean Paul, or the great-but-doomed Heinrich von Kleist, or Johann Peter Hebel, or perhaps even Adalbert Stifter, he would not have written what is known to us as the categorical imperative, but a character who would have more or less resembled the categorical imperative. We can therefore think of literature and philosophy, and yes, even math, as expressions of the same basic human instinct. But one must remember: they are mere stories—total fictions—and nothing more."

I adjusted myself on my seat, trying to find more comfortable purchase, as if I were settling in at a theater.

"Math is fake," Professor Aleister said, "but at least math is more real-fake than philosophy, which is fake-fake. Literature of course is fake-real. Even the total failures of literature—pharmacy-store paperbacks, amateur work of the poorest caliber— even these examples are more fake-real than the most sublime work of philosophy, which is always fake-fake. I've dedicated my life to boring nonsense, it seems, I would say, when I should have dedicated my life to *delicious* nonsense. Boring nonsense has no redeeming qualities. But delicious nonsense at least tastes good. Yes, you can masticate delicious nonsense. It tastes good and you can swallow it after a good chew. Boring nonsense leaves your stomach grumbling. Or worse: it gives you a terrible ache in your gut. As if you had truly eaten something foul. And you have."

I went to grab for my beer bottle, which I had placed next to me on the dining room table, and somehow managed to tip it over. I jumped up to catch it before it crashed on the floor, which I managed successfully, but not without spilling beer all over myself and on the Professor's carpet. I shook my wet arms as if they were injured. The Professor all the while had not moved—he continued peering straight ahead, as if there were an invisible interlocutor sitting now where I had been sitting only seconds before. I went to the kitchen to dry myself with a towel, but after riffling through the Professor's kitchen drawers to find where one might be stored, found they were mostly empty. One drawer had a few plastic soy sauce packets and some disposable chopsticks still in their paper sleeves. It appeared that the Professor had gotten rid of his utensils and other kitchen ephemera. There was an unopened roll of paper towels in a cabinet which I used to pat down my arm. As there was no garbage can in the kitchen, I placed the wet paper towels on an empty windowsill. Outside, it was beginning to snow. It was cold enough to amass a thin, speckled layer on the Professor's backyard grass, but not so cold to lie on the brick pathway, which led to a small gazebo at the far end of the Professor's property. It was there where Robert and I would smoke our cigarettes when we'd spend an evening at this house, all those years ago—we were the sole smokers of our cohort, and it was in cigarettes that our friendship was forged, however weakly. And it was now, I found, that I oddly had the urge to smoke again. It was not something I often felt after I quit, but the image of that lonesome gazebo gave rise to a desire within me to light one of those fine objects

and spend the rest of my evening outside, underneath that gazebo, safe from the snow, puffing away.
And in fact, that is what I made to do: I exited the
house through the Professor's kitchen back door,
and ambled to the miniature gazebo outside. The
bench seat was cold. Robert and I would both cram
ourselves onto this very surface many years ago, and
smoke away, always in silence, as our friendship was
buffeted by the communal expression of our little
band, and could not withstand going without the
social tapestry that gave it birth. We had, at the
beginning, made feeble attempts at small talk, but
then soon after rid ourselves of this civic burden
and enjoyed our cigarettes in silence, puffing at the
same pace, as we both smoked the comparatively
long-lasting American Spirits. And now I smoked
that cigarette in my mind, and allowed the requisite eight minutes or so to pass. Once I was finished
with my mind cigarette, I made my way back to the
dining room and sat down again. The Professor had
not stirred.

"I first warmed to you, of course," he said, "because of your name. Before I even met you. I saw
your name on my class roster and I nearly had a
heart attack. The room quite literally spun before

me. How was it so? How could it be? That you share his name."

He paused, as if in deep thought, perhaps forgetting he had said this to me before, not only the first time I met him, in his classroom, but subsequently throughout our time together as teacher and student, and then as friends. He had maybe said this to me a dozen times.

"It's not such an uncommon name, no," he continued. "Here in the States, yes, fine, it's not terribly common. But in Spain, in Latin America, it's not an uncommon name. Indeed, your last name shares the alternate naming of the Spanish language, of course, Castilian. It's in fact quite a common name in Spain, yes. I'd guess one of the most common they might have. The surname itself, a classic Spanish surname. But to have that same name arrive in my classroom? Right before me? I translated this man, Sebastián Castillo, for years and years, and here his double arrives, sitting himself right in my classroom, waiting for me to teach him Augustine's *Confessions*, which, I could tell by your classroom participation, you did not actually read. That's fine. That's quite all right. We can't read them all. No! Not even in a classroom, when a book has been put to you by your teacher, I understand. At times one cannot even read those books. It simply isn't the right time. You should have read it, of course. You would have learned a lot. When Augustine steals his pears, when he says he did it for no other reason than to commit an evil deed . . . *It was foul, and I loved it. I loved my own undoing.* Yes, you could have learned quite a bit from that, and you did not. But I had written on this man, indeed, I had dedicated a good many years of my life to translating Sebastián Castillo, and bringing his massive decades-spanning notebooks into the English-speaking fold, as it were. They were, admittedly, not even so popular in his home nation—hermetic, ant-size, illegible script written on napkins and other stray pieces of garbage. But, of course, I did meet his widow, and we both spent a good many hours combing through his archives. I had, years prior, read a small sample of his work—for only a sliver of his total notebooks had even been published in Spain—and there was something there worth capturing, worth pouring oneself into. I felt then that a bilingual edition of his work was necessary: it would be the push Castillo's work would need to gain the sort of repute I believed it deserved. When I flew to Menorca to sort through his archives, his widow kept thanking me in between each document. She quite literally would say 'Thank you so much,' in English, after I read each page of Castillo's notebooks, and various addendums, which his widow had dutifully not only kept, but organized for me chronologically. She would sit next to me as I worked, and I would turn a page, and she would say 'Thank you so much.' The truth was that she thought publishing her late husband's work into English would mean lots and lots of money," the Professor said. He laughed so loudly that I jumped. "She thought it meant a big pile of money! That's what she thought. She was quite old then, and living off a pension, not unhappily, I don't think. But she wanted a great deal of money. I had to remind her that I was getting paid very little for my work—even my trip to Spain, to the island of Menorca, was not covered by the university or the prospective publisher. I paid for it all out of my own pocket: to come to Menorca to sort through this dead man's work. Franco had just died and there was something celebratory in the air, though I could have been imagining it. I am wont to imagine things very easily, as you know, and it's possible I'm imagining there was a celebratory spirit in the air, or if I, merely myself, was feeling celebra-tory, as Franco was finally dead and in the ground, and very hopefully burning in Hell, for all eternity, where he belongs, and of course I was also feeling quite sanguine about finally having access to Cas-tillo's papers. Castillo himself, of course, was no fas-cist, but he was no anarchist or communist either, no. His commitments and whereabouts during the Spanish war are totally unknown, but we can probably guess: he was a man who dedicated his life to obsessive reading and shutting out the world outside his bedroom window completely. So while his country was being torn apart, he was probably reading a book. In that sense, he was a writer in the tradition of Pessoa or Borges—both the good and bad in those men, and maybe especially the bad. To be frank, I was surprised he had managed to marry. But yes, his widow thought that the work of her dear, late husband would amount to a large golden coin she'd be able to slip into her coffer. No such luck, of course. I practically had to beg magazines to review this translated notebook in English. The problem was that no one read those magazines, and the few people who did, did not read the re-views of Sebastián Castillo's notebooks. I recall one such magazine wrote a three-sentence review in a side column, describing Castillo as a 'Balearic hermit' whose work was 'puzzling at best.' I had originally intended to publish these bilingual editions of his notebooks in three volumes—the project really called for five or six volumes, but I compromised with three—and the publisher canceled the contract after the first volume sank like a stone in the Mediterranean. The public would have to make do with a single volume, which covered only the early period of his thought—of a much different character than his later period, which is decidedly more cryptic. But yes, 'puzzling at best,' that's all they said. I tried for years to usher who I thought was a wonderfully esoteric obsessive of letters into the pantheon. But, well, no, that didn't quite work. No. The publisher stopped responding to my queries. I didn't even receive the second half of my translator's advance, a pittance as it was. I suppose they wanted to recoup some of their loses. After years of trying, I gave up on this man's work. I put it behind me. I let it steam in the past. And then what? Then you show up to my classroom door, on my roster. Sebastian Castillo, without the accent on the *a*. It was as if that man's ghost was coming to me. As if he was saying: not good enough. You did not put in the requisite effort. Well, I did. There was nothing that could be done about it," he said.

I had the thought to tell the Professor that he had told me this story already. That he had told me a variation of this story several times throughout our relationship: that I could, if I wanted, recite every biographical detail of this obscure and, to be frank, utterly mediocre writer because I had been bludgeoned into remembering those details. I felt so irritated at having to share a name with this man—this epigone of, yes, Pessoa and Borges and perhaps even Beckett, that I went so far as to adopt as a nom de plume for my own published work—I wanted nothing to do with him, no association with this failed and entirely rightly forgotten Spanish philistine. I remember once, when the Professor was regaling me with this story for the umpteenth time, he demanded I commit to memory everything I could about this man, who was, after all, so he said, my double. He told me I had an ethical—if not spiritual—obligation to remember everything I could about Sebastián Castillo, who spelled his name with an accent, even though I didn't. There had to have been a reason I was given the name I had been given, he said, and I was lucky enough to find that reason, so I should commit to it. The Professor insisted I begin writing my name with an accent; he said it was necessary I do this. And ultimately, I did, in fact. I became Sebastián, yes. But for reasons completely unrelated to him, to this, to the Professor's asinine injunctions.

It was then, sitting in the Professor's dining room, listening to the Professor once more, recalling these conversations over the years, that I felt a fury rise within me. Maria was not coming. Robert and Thomas or even Roger or Max, his simpering assistant, were not coming. The Professor had not planned a party after all. He had ensnared me; he had engineered a trap that would make it so that I would return to his house. Abruptly, I rose and walked back into the living room and up the stairs, toward the Professor's bathroom on the second floor. I didn't excuse myself. As I ascended the stairs, I could see that Professor Aleister's gaze had not changed. He peered forward as always. His eyes did not meet mine as I ascended the stairs. In his bathroom—which was, oddly, rather well kept—I sat on the Professor's commode for a good half hour. I searched for an excuse to leave. I didn't *need* an excuse, to be sure—I had been tricked into coming here, into spending my New Year's Eve with this moribund, raving fool. In front of the toilet there was a side table of sorts, atop of which were a number of wrinkled magazines—*Time*, *Life*, *Harper's*. I looked through them; all were several years old. At the bottom of the pile there was a book: *Letters to a Young Poet* by Rainer Maria Rilke, a book I had always found sentimental and undeserving of its reputation. I remembered then a line from the great Swiss writer Robert Walser, on Rilke: "Bedtime reading for old maids." I flipped through the volume and to my astonishment discovered it was a first edition English-language copy of the book. It would be worth at least a thousand dollars, if not more, and here it was, next to his toilet, buried under musty, creased magazines. The book itself was in fine condition. I would not leave the Professor's house empty-handed, I decided. More than anything, I badly needed the money: I had no intention of returning to teaching, and my savings were at this stage, given my yearlong sabbatical from life, next to nothing. Affordable as my apartment was, and as ascetic as my purchasing habits could be, I was but one accident away from complete financial insolvency. I slipped the book into my jacket pocket and headed back downstairs. The Professor was seated as before, though now he was holding a book in his hands. I sat down across from him again, readying myself to announce my departure. The book he was holding was titled *Deleuze for Dummies*.

"I have never understood Deleuze, no," Professor Aleister said. "I have made a great effort trying to understand him. I have read a great deal of his books. I have read, several times, his *Anti-Oedipus*, written along with that Guattari. I've read that book at least three or seven times. And I cannot claim to understand a word of it. I've read, much more I might add, Foucault's introduction to that book, on how to live the anti-fascist life, and I admit that introduction has at times, on certain afternoons, filled me with something close to hope, and perhaps even filled me with the desire to continue forth in the matter of life. But when I open the pages of Deleuze and Guattari, while I laugh at what they have to say—for they are quite funny, I admit—I do not understand a single world of it. I do not know what they mean. And I don't understand Deleuze because I don't understand Spinoza, of course, for Spinoza is Deleuze's guide, as much as Virgil guides

Dante, there is no doubt of that. We know they are both right—Deleuze and Spinoza—one knows this, though one doesn't understand Deleuze, and one can never understand Spinoza. What each says is perfectly true, and beyond reproach. They are perfect philosophers. But it is not clear what it is either have said, it's true. The only thing I understand of Deleuze is that he killed himself when he was already quite old. That I understand. He, as they say, defenestrated himself. He threw himself out the window. Now, to defenestrate oneself is no small suicide. That is making quite the show of it. One looks out one's bedroom window. The rain patters lightly upon one's bedroom window. One has all manner of deep thought while gazing out one's bedroom window, and one even writes poetry on the occasion. But one does not throw oneself out one's bedroom window, unless of course you really want to make a *big splash*. But it seems to me that Deleuze was not one to make a big splash. No. I can't claim to understand a word of his writing, I admit this freely, but I respect him. I respect Deleuze. Derrida, Lacan, I don't respect. I think of them as fools. Yes. Derrida and Lacan are professional wrestlers. Not serious thinkers, no. Derrida might have a few good moments, but never Lacan. He is merely a performer. His lectures are laughable, or rather, they would be laughable if you didn't want to cry while watching them. Or throw up, really. A lout, that man. Disgusting. I feel sick to my stomach thinking about him, and the things he said, and how awful, sheep-like people somehow seem to take him seriously. Freud was a real thinker, and what's more, an excellent writer. A truly polyvocal, mellifluous writer of prose. But Lacan was neither. They should have shot him. If Lacan were sitting in front of us, and I had a revolver in my hand, I would blow his brains out. A bullet in the head would have solved the problem of Lacan," he said.

I tried to interrupt his speech, for it seemed he was only getting started. This was a performance to which I had been a captive audience many times, and understood that one must find their way out when the opportunity arises—the pauses in his speech the gate through which the Messiah, my exit, might enter. But I was once again arrested by his dialogue.

"The only thing I understand about Deleuze is that he killed himself. I think anyone with even a shred of self-respect should probably do the same once they've approached the requisite age, yes. One

should not do so when they are too young—that is
letting death eat fruit none too ripe. But once one
has reached the requisite age, yes, that's the only
acceptable way to go. My wife, for instance. Yes.
That's what she did, as it were. As I discovered.
Though she was long retired she announced to
me one day she had to travel back to Spain to help
some firm on consulting business. She was heading
to Barcelona, and was to be there for three days. On
that third day she phoned to say that she was, to
my surprise, in Mahón, on Menorca. She thought
she'd return to the town of her childhood, she said
to me over the phone. Her family hadn't lived there
in quite some time, and there weren't very many of
her relatives left—a few cousins, though they now
all either lived in Barcelona proper or along the
Catalonian coast. Of course, as you can imagine,
it is in Mahón, on Menorca, where I met her, on
my trip, my *translation trip*. I still remember that
day: I stopped at a café, a hole in the wall, a place
to get a caña and a plate of olives, and she was my
waitress. I took to her immediately. Well, I won't
go for retelling the old courtship story. But yes,
I went to Menorca to begin my translation work
on the writer with whom you share a name, and I

myself was transformed, as it were, from a bachelor into a married man. And when Isabella was in Barcelona, she phoned to say to me: I'm going back to my childhood. That is what she said. Not her childhood *home* or her childhood *town* but her childhood itself. This was about a year ago now, yes. I found it odd, certainly, but I did not object. Our money, after all, is really *her* money, and I was never in the position to tell her how to spend it. She was the breadwinner; I was a lowly college professor. I told her to phone me once she had arrived, but she never did. Or at least, the phone call I received was not from her, but from the island authorities, calling to inform me that my wife was now dead. She had hung herself in her hotel room. My wife, my dear Isabella, had spent a single day in Mahón—she had returned to her essential site, something private, which I could not quite know myself, and she decided she had had enough of the whole business of living. The authorities, over the phone, had told me that housekeeping found her hanging in the closet. A young boy, they said. I've never been able to understand why the Menorcan authorities included that detail in their report to me, that a very young boy who had just started working at the hotel was the one to discover her body. I felt, then, that I was being made to feel guilty, somehow. That my wife, and by proxy, I, had traumatized a lowly sort of working-class Balearic boy from the provinces. I declined to have her body shipped back to the States. I informed her cousins in Barcelona and asked that they hold the funeral there, and that I would be in Barcelona as soon as I could. But I never went. I stopped receiving phone calls from her family and I did not go to Spain. I don't know what happened," he said. "And what do I imagine she did there, on her last day? Isabella's family had owned a dairy farm on the island, stretching back generations, though she herself was not a farmer, let me assure you. And on that dairy farm, her parents had a paddock in which they kept donkeys, for they felt that the keeping of the meek and gentle donkey was something they ought to do. And it's there, I remember Isabella telling me, in that very paddock, where her parents had died. Of what, I had never ascertained: whenever I would inquire on the matter, she had said that something awful, something so terrible, had happened there in that paddock, that she could never speak of it aloud. This occurred when she herself was a young girl. That is, both of her parents, they both had died in that donkey paddock, when she was but a child. And of what they had died—whether they had been executed by the police or the military or a gang, or, it seems possible, by the donkeys themselves—I never did learn. I stopped broaching the subject after our first few years, as she would wave her hand and say: Something had occurred there of which she could never speak, could never utter aloud, and so the subject was kept away in the past. And so I imagine that Isabella had visited that paddock, had seen the site of her childhood, her childhood itself, and from there on decided that after witnessing this image once more, it was the end. That's what I imagine. In fact, I'm certain."

The Professor flipped through the pages of *Deleuze for Dummies* and placed it down on the dining room table. He stood for the first time since I'd arrived, and hobbled over to a closet behind him, from which he removed a suitcase and a cardboard box. He placed both of these items beside his chair and sat down again.

"I emailed the school and told them I'd be unable to return," the Professor said. "It was long past time for retirement, and I could dedicate my days to translation and to writing. Though in fact I have done no such thing."

I stood to leave. The Professor's arm shot up at me, dangling in the air with what felt like to me a preternatural force, and in response, I sat back down.

"Three weeks ago," Professor Aleister said, "I received an email from my son's wife, to whom I had not spoken in several years, as I had not spoken to my son in several years. My wife maintained a relationship with him, but I did not. Too much had passed between us. A rupture that had developed and festered for years had grown ever more gangrenous. Something uncrossable had established itself between us. In his youth it was drugs and drinking and then it was his religious fanaticism. And then perhaps later it was merely an issue of personality. We did not like each other. I did not like him. And so we ceased speaking. If I am at fault, and I suppose I am in a small way, it is because I did not report to him the death of his mother. He found out from a relative in Barcelona. And due to my negligence, though it was perhaps an *intentional* negligence of which I was not aware, he had missed the funeral, and he was upset about this. About missing his mother's funeral, because her family there assumed

I had informed him, when I hadn't. He flew to Barcelona to collect her ashes, apparently, and it was there he had a relapse of sorts, I suppose, for, as his wife—I suppose *surviving wife*—told me, he had indeed overdosed there in Barcelona. Whether or not it was intentional it was not possible to say, though it seems it was an accident. His wife—rather, *surviving wife*—said this to me over an email, you see," the Professor said, and for the first time in the evening he tilted his head away from me, breaking our eye contact. "I remember when he was sixteen or seventeen, out of a rehabilitation facility for the second time, how he converted to Catholicism, which felt even more putrid to me than when I had first discovered cocaine in his room. We didn't raise him as anything. We were the consummate secular family in the suburbs. And then one day he begins speaking about how Christ is his salvation, and about the Church and its vicar. He blamed me for not teaching him Augustine and Duns Scotus, and how massively all of this was to change his life. It seemed to me he lacked an essential understanding of the world, of why he felt the compulsions he did, how miserable it all made him, and that an essential understanding was delivered to him through this belief. I don't think it was deeply sincere, no. It merely offered an alternative path to quell some deep ignorance within him: Why do I do these things? It seemed he had asked himself. Why? And the Catholic Church's teachings provided him some salutary response. At least he didn't become a Protestant," the Professor said. "His wife's— *surviving wife's*—email said: I do not believe he took his own life. Those are the words she used. Took his own life. I found the choice amusing—he should have taken his own life many more times than he did, of course. He was always being led by someone or something else, which I had always found dismal, disappointing. My own son! Too bad he had not committed suicide, at least I could have been proud of him for something."

The Professor stood and walked slowly into the kitchen. I thought of leaving without saying good-bye. I felt so put upon by his story—so deeply used as a member of his audience—that I recognized the urge within myself, distantly, for physical harm. I wanted to slap this man and tell him that he was the sole judge, jury, and executioner of his life's problems, and that if tragedy had befallen him, it was his fault and his fault alone. *No wonder your wife killed herself!* I wished to say. The cardboard box he had brought out of the closet sat half open next to his chair. I opened it. It was filled with cash. All stacks of banded hundred-dollar bills—there was easily well over half a million dollars, if not much more. I must have felt guilty of trespass, for as soon as I heard the Professor skulking back, I hastily closed the cardboard box and resumed my position in my chair. The Professor returned with a bottle of Yuengling in his hands, and sat back down.

"It's my life savings," the Professor said, "or rather, my wife's life savings. You should see what I have left over from all those years working at the university. I could probably buy a donkey with it, but not much more. And then where would I keep it? I liquidated all accounts, all assets, all stocks and certificates of deposit. That's all of it. I'm giving it away."

I tried to offer a laugh in response, but what emerged from my throat was an inchoate, awkward noise. The Professor remained impassive.

"I remember you always with something or other about New Year's resolutions," he said. "I remember you talking about it *ad nauseam*—the sanctity of, the necessity of, a New Year's resolution. You were going through a phase with the Stoics, I remember, with Epictetus and Marcus Aurelius. Constant vigilance. Total self-mastery. More indifference to indifferent things. Every young man such as yourself has such a mistaken phase. He has such a phase, and he commits himself to little rules and so on. More rules to follow! No eating after seven o'clock. Water first thing in the morning. One hundred push-ups a day. A young man such as yourself has such a mistaken phase and it is a thing to observe. Like watching a dog chase its tail: look at how diligently he applies himself. Or rather, I should say, a donkey chasing the apple dangled before its muzzle. But this year, I think I'll follow suit myself. I've finally come around to it. To making a resolution. I am going to fly to Menorca and kill myself, as my wife did before me. I could very well do it here, of course, but then some awful suburban police officer who has never read a page of Kant in his life would find my corpse. Some idiot, twentysomething police officer who has never even read the preface to Kant's first critique. I'm not so sure I want such a man to be the person to have the gift of seeing my corpse for the first time. No—in Menorca, in my *translation project*, I was translated from a bachelor into a married man. And there I'll return and translate my body into death, as it were. So no, I can't do it here, that won't do. I've always despised the suburbs; it has been my life's damnation to live in one, I would at the very least like to die elsewhere. I'll have to do it on Menorca, a perfect place to kill yourself, it must be said. And besides, the only people in my life, both of whom have gone before me, chose Spanish soil for their deaths, so why not myself. Well, at least my wife chose. Spanish soil—or rather, *Menorcan* soil—seems a good soil for killing oneself. The climate is dry—it doesn't get too cold. So yes, I'll take a flight next week or so, once I've finished handing out this money, once I have a few bits and bobs in order, and I'll take a room in a hotel in Menorca, and get on with it. That's what I'll do. That's what I'd like to do," he said. He paused. A long silence passed between us.

"And why shouldn't I do it?" the Professor asked. "If one of life's chief goals is to prepare oneself for death, then I should say I am sufficiently prepared. I am old. There is no one left in my life. I had to bribe you here, didn't I? I'm not so dumb. I didn't know if you would come, to be sure, I didn't know if that sort of phase had passed with you, but I knew I touched on the right corner of your life, didn't I? And here you are: you have sat here dumbly, searching for an excuse to leave the entire time so you could go home, get drunk alone, and play with yourself. And lacking the constitution to say even a single word to me, you have failed. Look at you. So, again, why shouldn't I do it?"

The Professor opened the suitcase that sat next to the cardboard box. Within it there lay a coil of rope, at the end of which was a noose.

"Look, I've already packed my bags!" the Professor said. "I've no need for anything other than the clothes on my body, after all. They won't let you on the plane naked, no. I'll go through the TSA and put my suitcase through their scanners, and they'll ask, *Sir, why are you traveling with a noose in your suitcase? The only thing in your suitcase is a noose.* And I'll respond: I am going to kill myself in Spain obviously! And they'll have no choice but to accept my resolve and let me board the plane. One TSA officer might make a joke about my using the rope as a lasso on one of the other innocent fliers, and I'll say I'm much too old for that anyhow, bothering people with my little games and diversions, and then he'll say something or other about how I should have a nice suicide, and I'll say, Oh yes, I'm planning on having a lovely suicide, and he'll say the weather in Spain is indeed lovely for hanging yourself, and I'll say that's exactly why I'm going there! The weather for suicide!"

The Professor removed a bundle of cash from the box and played with its edges, like playing cards.

"My boy," he said, "take a nice sum of this. I know the life of an academic is thankless, and what's more, they don't pay you for the pleasure."

He placed what was likely twice my annual salary in cash on my lap. I stared down at it as if the sum threatened me. It was all of the world in a bundle of lousy paper. And someone had made me like it.

"I've already given away a large chunk of it," he said, "so even if I were to change my mind, I would become destitute, and they'd have to cart me off to somewhere that would become my grave anyhow. I suppose I could always go the route of a Grothendieck and become a wild hermit, living on the heath. Surviving off grass and berries. Settle in filth in a hole in the ground. But no: I'm much too old for that now. There's no turning back for me."

I wanted to tell him to not do it. Or rather: I felt compelled to—I didn't know whether that suggestion arose from a sincere impulse, and the thought

felt too depressing to pass through my thoughts beyond the image of generic concern.

"I'm sure you will say that I should continue
living. That I should continue living, and that I
shouldn't do this. I have something to live for, you
feel like saying. But don't you have anything else to
contribute? I am disappointed. One would hope that
a person such as yourself would have a more useful
perspective to contribute. I thought that maybe we
could drink to my suicide. I was hoping you would
wish me a good suicide, or that you would say, perhaps, I was going to have one of the best suicides, that
no one would do it like me. Not merely an exemplary
suicide: a legendary suicide! But no. I shouldn't do
it, I'm sure you'd like to say. Are you not a writer of
little moral fables? Are you not capable of offering
something a bit more unique than bromides given
the circumstances? Surely you are better than the
speech of an automaton. You could deliver a more
convincing performance, no? And I've seen you do
it! So why not rally yourself and provide us with
something a bit more palatable than: you should live.
No, I shouldn't," the Professor said.

I stood and placed the mounds of cash on the seat
of my chair. I walked over to the bookshelf next to

the dining room table. I didn't know why I had done it—why I had stood, and why, at that moment, I had decided to pretend to scan the titles of the books the Professor kept in this room. Having started, however, I felt the need to see the motion to its end, as if to suggest I had done this with intention, as opposed to having done it randomly, for I didn't know what else I should do. I had often behaved quite like this: in certain difficult situations, I would begin doing some distracted movement or activity as if I were preoccupied with another matter—something I had forgotten until the present moment—that I needed to take care of right away, for whatever reason. I pressed my hand on the spine of a withering, dust-covered book: Jean de la Bruyère's *Characters*—the Penguin paperback edition—and made as if to remove it but pressed it back into its slot. I drummed my fingers against the spine and a small cloud of dust wafted from it, toward me.

"You should like to help me, I'm sure you think," Professor Aleiester said. "But you don't know how. Do you? You don't know anything about that. You've never known anything."

I returned to my seat and stuffed the bundle of cash into my jacket pocket. I walked into the living room. The Professor remained in his seat, gazing back toward me in much the same way he had throughout the evening. I met his gaze and returned it. I made my way back to his entrance room, stepping atop the dried, crunchy leaves of his dead plants, and left his house.

Immediately, I was shivering. It had gotten much colder in the intervening two or so hours I had been at the Professor's, and the snow had begun to accumulate on the sidewalk, making my walk back to the station more difficult than I had expected. My thighs felt cold, and despite my walking at a faster and faster pace—I was practically speed walking, at times almost slipping on the compacting snow—I could not warm them. I must have registered as a curious figure to the cars passing me by: a young man speed walking in the quiet, night-dead suburbs of Philadelphia on New Year's Eve. A few of these cars began honking at me, and I thought maybe they were encouraging my behavior—admiring my mirthful, erratic walking. Feeling something like a circus jester seeking to please my audience further, I made my walking all the more outrageous, tilting my torso backwards as I sauntered to the regional rail station, kicking out my legs exaggeratedly as if I were warding off something invisible accosting me along my journey through the night. I looked like that picture of John Lennon walking strangely. Brief clouds of snow exploded into the air with every jostling of my leg. After I had done this for some time, it occurred to me to check my phone for the coming, scheduled train. I had no messages. Who would message me? It was a few minutes past midnight: the cars were honking to wish me a happy New Year's. I arrived at the station out of breath, and only a few minutes before the next train back into the city. I had also arrived at that which I had planned for myself a year prior: I spent an entire year without saying a word out loud to a single person.

On the train, remembering I had stolen the Professor's copy of *Letters to a Young Poet*, I removed the book from my bulging jacket pocket and began flipping through it. I had on me probably one hundred thousand dollars in cash. The book had been inscribed to someone, which I hadn't noticed when I first glanced through it on the toilet—not the Professor, for the inscription was dated 1934, which would have been, I believed, a few years before the Professor had been born—no, this inscription was for its first recipient. It read: "To T. for T." and in smaller handwriting there was written: Christmas Day, 1934. So this book was a Christmas present, likely from one older man to a younger man, and here it was, nearly a century later, stolen from one older man and returned into the hands of a younger man. I had read the book years ago, on the recommendation of a teacher—not the Professor—who said it gave her the necessary courage to write poetry. I found that laughable once I actually read the book, this lamentable exchange of letters, where the young supplicant hopes to receive some encouragement on his middling verse, and some greater words of hope and wisdom from the learned master, who, knowing his vaulted position in this young tadpole's mind, takes great pleasure in doling out his well-earned tutelage, going so far as to dip into vulgar sentimentality—*if one could not write, one would die*! I found myself laughing aloud as I read the book, laughing at an erratic and sensational pitch, so much so that the two other passengers in my car on the regional train back into the city looked over at me. One took out a little flask and downed a bit more of whatever they had stored there. The second traveler in my cart gave me pause. She was at its opposite end—I hadn't noticed her until that moment, slightly shaded as she was. Often these regional trains, especially in the late evenings, would either partially lose power—and therefore the entire car would be shrouded in darkness—or they would intentionally dim their lights to offer late-night passengers some tranquility. She looked up at me, in the midst of my sensational laughing, and I could register the momentary apprehension of recognition followed by a deflected glance outside her window. She was now in profile, with the moon's light acknowledging her face. It was Maria. She had seen me and, immediately, hoping I had not recognized her, turned her face toward her train window, gazing at the rolling suburbs outside, and the New Year's moon above it. She was wearing a different outfit from what she had posted a few hours ago: she was now in a red dress with black shoes. Her Guermantes best. There she was: Maria. Had she dressed so as an act of reclamation? Returning to the lightly gone past, with the hope of rekindling what was not possible before? Perhaps she had dressed as she was, full of determination to weather the Professor's onslaught once more, with the hope of seeing me, knowing how much delight I would find in that gesture. And then, at the final moment, she had decided against it. No—she could not return to it. Too much had passed, and too long. She thought it would be foolish. And now Maria was likely off to an event in the city, at a friend's place, perhaps, or maybe to a Center City after-hours club. She knew it was me. And she was not going to say hello. I spent the remainder of my train ride wondering if I should say something, if I should approach her, given that I had planned my entire evening with the hope that I could see her once more, for the first time in many years, and here she was, a mere twenty feet away from me. But it was clear that she did not wish to say anything to me, no, she wished to continue the silence between us indefinitely. She had remained in profile all this while, slightly shaded as she was, and then finally turned to her phone, whose light illuminated the more delicate features of her face. Now her face was finally on view. Except, where Maria's thick brown eyebrows were supposed to be, there were manicured, threaded eyebrows—thin like em dashes. And where Maria's vulpine nose should have been, there was something nubby and flat. This woman was wearing Maria's dress, her Guermantes best, but it was not her. No, it was not Maria. After shutting off her device, the woman stood and walked to the car behind her. She was looking for a bathroom.

During my transfer from the regional rail to SEPTA, I found myself moving about in an irregular, desultory fashion. It was only after a few blank moments that I realized I was experiencing an episode of dissociation—I felt as if I were watching myself wander through the underground station, and it dawned on me that I didn't know what I was doing, or where I was going—the landscape before me had lost all sense of recognition. What was once a familiar Philadelphia set-piece had become a collection of images without reference: color and line swam in front of my face as if in mockery. I thought to speak to who I believed was a man sleeping on the floor, but he was a slab of cardboard. He was merely cardboard. There was no one. I could not find it possible to produce noise from my mouth, despite that new possibility which I had been granted at midnight. I had begun then to experience the beginnings of a panic attack—before I was wont to exercise, before I had taken the utmost concern with my health, I was accosted by these attacks regularly, when the world would flatten before me, a sensation of prickling enveloped the back of my head, and I began sweating profusely. During these attacks it felt that my life was finally over, that everything had led me to this moment when the world would tuck itself away and I would die alone somewhere within it. These attacks were largely the product of the minor heart scare I had experienced, a heart scare that I should not have experienced at my age. For the first time in years, it felt like an attack of this nature was returning to me—returning home—well after I thought I had resolved my problem. I could feel my chest tighten and my heart patter furiously with me. I could no longer breathe. My face and neck grew hot, and it was as if I needed to escape out of my very body lest I be struck down by something unimaginably horrendous. I then remembered a line from Descartes—a philosopher whom I have always typically disliked, and who previously had never offered me the slightest consolation: if one is lost in a forest and one has no idea which way to go, one should go straight ahead because it is not likely worse than anything else. And I proceeded as such, in a sprint. It was just my luck that this was precisely the direction that was designed for me, and indeed where I needed to travel should I meet the subway that would take me back to my house. I descended that necessary staircase and, as earlier in the evening, the subway was pulling into the empty station as I arrived to meet it.

Once on the subway, with the coolness of the seat chilling my bottom, I performed a breathing exercise with my eyes shut closed. A minute and twenty seconds passed—the length of this numbing exercise, and I could feel the world return to me in its dumb normalcy: from inscrutable pain back into common boredom. My subway car was empty; it was, after all, almost one in the morning, albeit on New Year's Eve, or, I suppose, now New Year's Day proper. I found myself, having calmed myself down from my panic episode, teeming with a capacious sense of irritation. Typically, when these episodes abated, I could only manage to summon a feeble gratefulness that it was over. But this time was different; my annoyance had expanded beyond the boundaries of what had just happened in my evening, toward everything that had ever happened in my life: of all the turns in the road of living I had taken, those turns had led me here, despite all my efforts, at this precise moment, in this empty, stale subway car in the middle of the night, alone and shaken. It seemed impossible, but it had happened.

The subway door opened at a stop—which I couldn't see—and a youth of about eighteen or nineteen years entered. He sat directly across from me, despite the fact that the entire car was empty. He looked about the age of one of my students—college freshman, more or less still high school students who happened to be attending a university. They needed yet a proper year of the experience to move beyond the picayune affectations of childhood. He was one of these young men who, despite the cold, do not wear jackets. Perhaps they all want to advertise their masculine indifference to such insignificant concerns such as the weather. This young man wore an oversized sweater, and on his shoulder slung a tote bag with a famous Japanese cartoon character drawn on the side. He wore a thin mustache and had loose, curly hair on the top of his head, though the sides were shaved. Plugged into his ear were white wireless headphones, the kind my students wore all the time. We made eye contact briefly and when I registered a slight shock in his face, I realized it was because I had been crying, and tears streaked my cheeks. He removed a book from his bag and began reading. It was a popular book—one written by a right-wing pseudo-intellectual who advocated for traditional, conservative perspectives on the garden variety of issues that might interest an audience of mostly young men who looked exactly like this boy sitting before me. Things like: our current age's loss of masculinity; liberal culture's obsession with sensitivity; and the appropriateness of gender roles that produced the kind of society in which this pseudo-intellectual wished to live. This man had become famous because he had engaged in a number of televised debates where he would speak quickly and harshly and with a certain tendentious, assured pomp about one issue or another, all the while his more liberal interlocutors would visibly grow angrier at this tedious man's blandly fascistic opinions of how the world should be run, and for whom. That anger would serve as evidence for fans of this pseudo-intellectual: how deeply ashamed and frustrated these liberal interlocutors were! With their gender studies patina! Look at how they fail in the face of real rationality, these young men seemed to think. It was all obvious to them. This pseudo-intellectual was one of many of these unfortunate media commentators who had become popular in the last half decade whom I deeply detested—not just for their various idiotic, jejune positions on the world, but because of the many fans they had accumulated—duped, really—who had convinced themselves they were geniuses by dint of listening to these worthless media personalities blather on. A veritable cottage industry had developed among these media personalities. And their fans—all of whom were young men—were utterly moronic and concept-thin, and the more fanatical of their number had even taken to forming small coteries of violent, right-wing social clubs who would often show up at various protests, ready to bash in anyone's skull who didn't look like them.

I stood and approached this young man. He gazed up at me, at first with an expression of defiance, it seemed, but then, quickly, I could see that this was a façade meant to protect himself: he was afraid. That irritation I'd felt before grew deeper, and by the time I was ready to produce words from my mouth, it had transformed into outright rancor. I said, "Do you think that the person who wrote this book, that such an awfully shallow, confused person could possibly teach you anything worth knowing? Do you think that telling you to make your bed in the morning is the kind of advice that should be printed in books and distributed internationally?

Do you think the nonsense this person claims to be the wisdom of the fucking sages is worth your time? Your precious, ever-dwindling time on earth? You understand, young man, that you will die someday—you will completely and permanently die, your body will desiccate—your *corpse*, rather— and that desiccation will in turn become a sorry collection of bone remains. That is your certain future, young man. And you think it's good to spend the rest of your short time on this planet reading books like this? Written by some completely horrid, flaccid epigone?"

I was out of breath as I had finished saying this. I could feel the veins in my body throb and push out against my flesh. I paused and, momentarily, tried to calm myself, but the attempt provided an opposite response, for I was even angrier than I had been preceding my speech. The boy stared up at me, frozen in horror. He had flanked the open book against his chest, holding it as if in defense against me, as if it were some sort of shield, as if I were but moments away from physically striking him. I had never hit a person in my life. I felt, at that moment, the urge to throttle his head as hard as I could manage against the subway railing. I wanted to mash his head so forcefully that his brain would shake against its container and inadvertently inspire some sense in this young man. I grabbed the book out of his hands and began ripping it in half. I feared that I would fail at this and subsequently look foolish and weak in front of this young person, but I was, to my surprise, entirely successful: I ripped his paperback in half and continued shredding pages from it. I then crumpled these pages into balls and threw them down the subway car's passageway, all the while the boy sat motionless in his seat. I had never in my life made someone so visibly afraid of me. There was little left of his book—the spine remained, and some tatterdemalion pages. I hoisted the book above my head, as if it were a wrestling partner, and with all my force I threw the book down at the floor below me.

"See?" I said.

I picked up the book up again, ripped out a few more pages, hoisted it above my head as before, and threw it down again with as much strength as I could manage. It bounced on the floor weakly and landed a few feet away.

"See?" I said, then retrieved the book and did this again, hoisting the book up in the air—more like an enemy's sword I had brandished against him, actually, than a wrestling opponent—and threw it again on the floor for the last time.

"Seeeeeee?" I said, making my voice large. I continued: "Do you think this fucking trash is worth your attention? This utter fucking trash? You would do better to buy a pound of hard drugs, right now, and snort them up into your face, than read a word this person has to say. That, I would say, would rot your brain considerably less than a single sentence form this utter fucking epigone of a human being. I mean, honestly, you would do better *picking random pills off the fucking street* and eating those pills than reading this book or watching this man speak in any of those videos of which I am sure you are quite the fan," I said.

I was shaking with a frenzy so savage it felt as if something in my nervous system was going to burst. The boy was crying. And seeing this, something softened within me, and indeed with that softening came a wave of recrimination for what I had just done. The boy hadn't said a word or raised his hands against me throughout the duration of my performance. He did not offer the slightest resistance. I didn't know what else to do.

"Here!" I said, and pulled Rilke's book out of

my jacket pocket, whereupon a stack of hundred-dollar bills fell to the floor. I crouched down and retrieved my money. "Here," I said, and placed the book in his hands. "Read this book. It will give you the necessary courage to write poetry. You will write poems, and you will stop reading books by that man. You will stop considering that man. You will write poetry instead, and you will need the necessary courage to do so. You will read about a man named Rilke, and you will be filled with courage. He was great, and you will know him. I've done you a tremendous favor," I said, and smiled at him manically. The young man received the book and offered a weak noise of gratitude in response. He surveyed the shredded balls of paper littered on the subway floor as if they were a beloved pet who had become rabid and subsequently been put down. I was its executioner. I looked out the train window—the subway had gone so far east that the El had emerged from the underground and was now elevated above Front Street, in Fishtown. I had missed my stop. I got off at Girard.

The street was empty. I stood alone on the corner of Front Street. The train above me headed north toward Berks. And it was then I remembered something: in the final sequence of my favorite movie, the titular character, a fifteenth-century Russian monk and painter of icons, takes a vow of silence as a means of punishing himself. He has done something he is convinced is unforgiveable, and believes the only way for him to address this sin is to cease speaking, and to cease painting. Years pass. He wanders. One day, he witnesses from afar a young boy, the supposed apprentice-son of a famed bell maker, digging on the foundry site for a brand-new bell, commissioned by the Grand Duke. This young man has promised certain important people he is capable of crafting this great bronze bell for the local church: he's claimed to the Grand Duke's subjects that his late father passed on to him *the secret of bell making*, and that therefore only he, this young peasant boy, is capable of constructing such a thing. But should he fail, the Grand Duke will have him beheaded—and not only him, but perhaps his entire crew. As he progresses on the bell, the young boy becomes increasingly despondent. Something is wrong. Andrei, the painter, continues watching him from afar—though he is silent, one can intuit he knows precisely what is happening: this young peasant boy has lied about his abilities.

He does not know anything about the building of bells, much less *the secret of bell making*. What's more, he has been foul with his crew, going so far as to having one of his workers flogged for a perceived lack of faith in his abilities. He has grown sick with a newfound, unearned authority. Eventually, the bell is cast and hoisted into its tower. All come to gather before the church—hundreds from the village, as well as all those who have helped create this fine object. The labor has been immense. The toil nearly unbearable. Finally, the Grand Duke and his retinue arrive. They await the bell's chime impatiently. The peasant boy knows his fate. It's over for him. Then something miraculous happens: the bell rings clearly. It should not have, but it has. All cheer. Our bell maker is huddled on the ground in tears. Andrei kneels and embraces him. The boy says, "My father, that old snake, didn't pass on the secret. He died without telling me. He took it to the grave." And our monk-painter, who has not spoken in years, says to him: "But you see, it turned out very well. Come on! What a feast day for these people! You've brought them so much joy, and you're crying. Let's go together, you and I. You'll cast bells, and I'll paint icons."

If only I had such work to do! And people in whom that work could grant a little bit of joy. Then, maybe, I could find something. I walked back home a long way in the snow, which cast itself generally over Philadelphia.

A Note on the Title and Chapters

THE TWO CHAPTER TITLES of this book are borrowed from *Loser* (2021) by Josef Kaplan. The title of this book comes from an 1836 lecture by the German writer Georg Büchner. I switched the order of adjectives because it sounded better. From "On the Cranial Nerves," translated into English by John Reddick:

> The search for such a law led automatically to those two wellsprings of knowledge that have ever been the heady drink of enthusiasts for absolute knowledge: the intuition of the mystic, and the dogmatism of the rationalist. As to whether it has ever proved possible to bridge the gulf between the latter and natural life as we directly apprehend it: any critique must answer no. A priori philosophy still dwells in a bleak and

arid desert; a very great distance separates it from green, fresh life, and it is highly questionable whether it will ever close the gap. Notwithstanding the intellectual finesse of its attempts to progress, it has to resign itself to the recognition that the points of its struggle lies not in the achievement of its goal, but in the struggle itself.

Acknowledgments

I would first and foremost like to thank my friends, without whom I would be nothing. I would also like to thank Alex Rubert, Mensah Demary, and Cecilia Flores for their editorial insights into this book. And thank you to everyone at Soft Skull who has made this a real, living object.

Sebastian Castillo is a writer and teacher living in Philadelphia. He was born in Caracas, Venezuela, and grew up in New York. His work has appeared in *New York Tyrant, Peach Mag, Electric Literature, Joyland, Epoch, BOMB*, and elsewhere. He is the author of *49 Venezuelan Novels, Not I, SALMON*, and *The Zoo of Thinking*.